C0-DVT-457

MURDER
FOR REASONS
UNKNOWN

MURDER
FOR REASONS
UNKNOWN

•

CAT LYONS

AVALON BOOKS
THOMAS BOUREGY AND COMPANY, INC.
401 LAFAYETTE STREET
NEW YORK, NEW YORK 10003

PRINTED IN THE UNITED STATES OF AMERICA
ON ACID-FREE PAPER
BY HADDON CRAFTSMEN, SCRANTON, PENNSYLVANIA

To Michelle, Christine,
Mike and Bette

Prologue

Her eyes misbehaved, darting back and forth: searching the garden shadows, peering into the many windows and doors of the great house. And always back to the pool. The three men swam toward her, a steady cadence of energetic splashes, gasping breaths, heads rocking, hands slapping. She kept her long legs draped over the pool rim, hanging in the water where Max could see.

In her mind the same thoughts flashed: this might never happen again, never a chance this good, the house empty, Lorenzo and Sam in the water with Max—when has that ever happened before—Miranda's day off, Louisa at the market shopping! It couldn't be better.

If not now, when?

Max was there before her. He grabbed her knee, squeezed it roughly. She recognized the gleam in his dark eyes, fueled by the thrill of the competition, the supreme confidence in victory. Lorenzo and Sam smacked the concrete on either side of her. Shoulder to shoulder the men turned. Like rockets they whooshed away from the end of the pool. Immediately Max regained a slim lead.

Mickey rose to her feet. She turned away and started walking, slowly at first, then briskly, along the winding mosaic inlaid path, ignoring the lush, beautiful garden. She didn't look back, but she was keenly aware of the steady rhythm of the swimmers' splashes, listening for any break, any clue that someone had noticed.

She was running when she reached the back of the house. The rhythm broke. The splashes seemed to grow loud, frantic, insistent. Mickey faltered, but no one yelled at her to stop. She listened, puzzled, but she didn't turn. Like a mountain climber refusing to look down, she wouldn't look back. Only an instant was lost. She hurried on. Jerking open the sliding glass door, Mickey fled into the house, grabbed her old canvas knapsack from a closet and ran through the cavernous front hall, expecting at every moment someone to appear and block her. Then she was out again in the brilliant sun. Heart pounding, she fled, down the broad steps, along the drive to the wall. One hand grasped the black steel of the wrought-iron gate. She threw her knapsack over. She clambered to the top, slipped, and fell to the ground, landing hard on her heels. She ignored the pain. Thirty feet along the hot cement sidewalk, she had managed to pull a yellow T-shirt over her head, over her wet bathing suit. Still running, she struggled into a pair of tan shorts and white sneakers.

At the corner luck was with her. A taxi! Almost hysterically, she waved and yelled. The taxi stopped.

"Aeropuerto," she gasped, piling in the rear. She looked back at the house, the stone wall, the wrought-iron gate, and was surprised to see—no one.

Chapter One

The burnished copper tangle of Mickey's thick, exuberant hair had lost much of its customary energy; where it fringed her forehead and framed her pretty face, damp dark tresses clung to her smooth golden skin. Under her arms and around her neck, down the middle of her front and back, shadows of sweat darkened her loose yellow T-shirt. Her bare arms and legs were slick and shiny.

Eleven miles in the blazing hot sun was a long trek, even for Mickey. She had walked this exact route before, on occasion, but not for many years. Back then the country road had been hard-packed gravel and the cars few and far between. It was long paved now; even the asphalt was sun-bleached gray and badly cracked by the bitter winter freezes. Cars whistled by but only

4

every couple of minutes. Mickey kept her thumb in the shoulder strap of her battered backpack, and, although she turned her head vigilantly to watch each car pass, she had no desire for a ride. She was more eager to get there than she had ever been, but this time she wanted to make the long journey on foot, to savor and explore each dusty recollection, to ease slowly back in time and properly prepare herself. Besides, she was more than a little afraid of the memories she might uncover.

Behind her she heard the throaty drone of an engine; a car noticeably slowed. Mickey angled farther away, well onto the ragged, weedy shoulder. She kept walking, twisting only her eyes back in a futile attempt to see behind, to know who it was. The car crept very close. It moved so slowly she could hear every loose stone groan beneath the crushing weight of the hot rubber tires.

Catching her breath, ready to flee, she looked. The car was beside her. She had to stop. Her body tensed. A male voice beckoned. "Mighty sticky day," he said as the window was rolled down in a series of jerks. "Can I give you a lift somewheres?"

Warily Mickey leaned forward to see the driver. She could feel the cold rush of air-conditioning caress her face. It was a stranger, an older man with a weathered, kindly face. With sudden relief she answered, "Thanks, but . . ." She hesitated, for a scant moment she considered abandoning her exhausting trek and accepting his invitation. It was almost too hot to breathe, no oxygen in the air, the air-conditioning was so wonderful, and she had nothing to fear from this man, but still she wasn't quite ready to be there, not yet.

"I really appreciate the offer, but I'm enjoying the walk." Then she nodded with a cordial smile.

The man slowly raised his hand, fist open. She could see he was surprised anyone would choose to walk on a scorcher like today. But he understood a young girl's reluctance to get in a car with a stranger. He gave a congenial wave. The car gradually accelerated and swung over onto the pavement. Mickey watched the car slide around a bend, then hop over a little rise and abruptly vanish. She was walking again.

More cars passed, but no other drivers stopped or slowed, or appeared to even notice her presence. She kept walking: a steady, even pace. The heat radiated up from the asphalt. Her mind meandered through thoughts of cool, refreshing plunges in the lake, delicious ice-cream treats from the Dairy Duchess in town, the faces of old friends and family, unrestrained laughter, parties on the sun deck, cozy fires in the fireplace, roaring bonfires on the stony beach, memories that made her happy as well as sad.

Close now, she turned away from the paved road onto one that led through a small marsh. This road was made of sand and loose stone packed down hard with deep damp ditches and tall bulrushes on either side. Another hundred yards and it scaled a small ridge, then split in two. Here even the gravel top changed to bare dirt. The empty fields gave way to smooth, bare rocks and scattered clumps of tall fir trees set in among walls of evergreen brush that partially concealed a dozen or so summer cottages. Most of the buildings were old and white clapboard with small windows and screened-in porches. There were several cottages she had never seen before, modern, light-stained wood with glass walls and vaulted ceilings peeking out in the gaps between the treetops.

The driveway Mickey entered was no more than two dirt grooves in the grass. It ran a short ways between bedraggled wild apple trees and petered out at the edge of a rough volleyball court with a tattered and cockeyed net. Ahead, beneath the drooping boughs of a huge old willow, there was the calm, beckoning lake. On the left was the cottage.

Each step forward caused an increase in the torrential flood of memories that accosted her. Her pace had gradually slowed. Her heart fluttered, and her green eyes grew wet and sensitive as she tried vainly to take it all in. The sudden desire to come back here—was it foolish? What did she hope to find?

The air hung still. Midweek, it was quiet, no one around; that much was a relief. She had been hoping she would be able to wander about freely. As each mile passed, each step, she had wanted, needed, these precious reflective moments more and more desperately.

Thankfully, the new owners had changed virtually nothing. That surprised her, for as much as she had considered the summer cottage absolutely perfect, she realized others might not.

A lot of changes can take place in eight years, Mickey reflected, calculating the time again. Eight years had flown by. She found it hard to believe it had been so long since her feet had trod the deep grass lawn. Indeed the grass was long, kept under control, but just barely. Cottage casual. It was more than ankle high. No one cared much about the weeds. Or the fact that maybe the wooden dock could use a fresh coat of paint to spiff it up. The cottage wasn't a place for finding work to do; though there needed to be a certain amount of upkeep, it had always been a place dedicated to fun and relaxation.

Mickey climbed up on the big cedar deck at the front. Even the wine barrel planters were still there overflowing with red and white geraniums. The deck furniture was new, but nice: solid redwood stained chairs and lounges with thick, gaily colored cushions, and a large table shaded by an enormous yellow umbrella.

To see in the sliding glass doors she held her hands up to shade either side of her face and pressed up against the glass. The drapes were open. The same big round table dominated the dining room. Deep in the dark background she just managed to make out the living area and the vast stone fireplace on the far wall.

If it hadn't been for a couple of little changes, it would seem so much like before that she could expect to see her mother coming out with a tray of cool watermelon slices, and her father rounding the corner in his white coveralls and baseball cap puttering around with a screwdriver, and maybe even Alan coming by in his boat to see if she wanted to go skiing. The thought made her spirits soar and sag again. Somehow, remembering the best of times only made the worst of times more poignant. Those wonderful days were gone. They could never happen again. A strange melancholy engulfed her—so happy and so sad at the same time. It kept her off balance. It scared her.

Turning abruptly, she hurried down to the stony beach and onto the dock. Kicking off her shoes, she sat on the very end, her feet dangling in the clear water. Consciously she took deep long breaths. She cried a little.

In the western sky the sun was starting to sink down upon the glimmering, still lake. Absently Mickey swirled her long legs in the cool water, and she followed the final descent of the sun as it nestled in behind the islands. It was peaceful. It was perfect. It was comforting.

What had happened to all the other people? she wondered. So many people had flowed through the cottage. Someone was always dropping in. Most summer weekends they would be bedding down a dozen or more friends or relatives, or just plain new acquaintances. Everywhere she looked memories of friendly faces appeared, invariably happily smiling back at her. Every memory—water ski tricks, silly dive contests, capsizing sailboats, games of charades, midnight swims, enormous barbecues—every memory that skimmed through her mind was joyous. Could it really have always been so happy here?

Suddenly dusk. No sign of a moon yet, but the first stars were sneaking through the opaque heavens. Reluctantly Mickey stood once more, tired, aware that she would have to make some arrangements for the evening. Twenty yards out, there was the old swimming raft. It was rocking gingerly in the wake of a distant, unseen boat. Then again, she mused, a little swim would feel exquisite. She wasn't carrying much but she did have her bathing suit, though it was still damp in the bottom of her knapsack. She looked around again. Impetuously she reached down and grabbed the hem of her T-shirt and drew it over her head. Mickey slid her shorts down her slender hips, then with her foot lifted them up to her hand. Why bother with a clammy swimsuit, she decided; after all, she was certain she was alone. Gathering together her knapsack and her discarded clothes she instinctively stuffed them beneath the little fiberglass sailboat that was overturned at the edge of the grass. Even the bright yellow sailboat was still there, exactly where it had always been, she noticed with amazement. This was where she used to hide her towel when she had gone skinny-dipping with her sister. Immediately she recaptured the youthful effervescence they had once felt—partly afraid someone would chance upon them—okay, if it was her mother, she might have joined in, but her father would have been mortified.

Casting a quick glance around, Mickey reassured herself she was still completely alone. She took two steps and leaped out, soaring, then stabbing into the water, radiating only a tiny round ripple in the surface and scarcely a splash.

Cool. Refreshing. Wonderful. The sticky grime of an exceedingly long day traveling was washed away. She continued underwater, pulling herself smoothly through the blackness, then burst to the surface, gasping for air. Joyously she filled her lungs, then swirled and wriggled like a frolicking seal.

At the raft she finally hoisted herself aboard, propelled up with a firm kick, then smoothly swung around in the air to sit, as though she had done it a thousand times before, which she probably had. Next, she leaned back, stretched out her long naked body, and lay staring up at the faint stars above.

The swim had been wonderful medicine, a calming sedative. Breathing deeply and slowly, she rocked with the imperceptible motion of the raft. Each breath came easier and slower than the last. There were many things Mickey had to think about, many decisions waited to be made, but she couldn't concentrate. She was tired. Thoughts just wandered aimlessly by, mixed with memories, flitting in and out of her consciousness. There was time to relax now and sort things out later.

When her eyes opened once more, she was staring up at a brilliant canopy of twinkling stars. She took a deep, delicious breath and stretched languorously again. Her tired muscles tingled in the cool, fresh air.

Suddenly the raft tipped. A spasm shuddered down her spine. A hand, a head, someone—a body, a man was heaving himself up right before her. A scream caught in her throat. Their eyes met. He fell back into the water. She rolled onto her stomach and hugged the rough wooden deck. Then, frozen—unable to speak, to move, to think—they waited.

"I'm . . . terribly . . . I didn't know." They both started at once. There was a splash, he was swimming away.

"Alan?" She knew it was him. Even before he spoke. Almost before she even saw him. Something in his motion, his aura. It could be no one but Alan, but surely it couldn't possibly be Alan.

In the sparkle of the starlight there was confusion, but shocked recognition. In the water, he stopped and turned his head toward her, then turned away before looking back once more.

"Mickey!" he said, incredulous.

She laughed.

He laughed nervously, the air bursting out from his

constrictive chest. "I don't believe this," he said, shaking his head.

Mickey flutter-kicked her feet playfully in the air. "I'd love to give you a great big hug, but . . ."

"I'll . . ." His voice faltered. "I'll look forward to that."

"So, how've you been, Alan?"

"Just great. How 'bout you?"

"Okay."

"It's been so long."

"Yes."

"I just can't believe you're here," he said, silently treading water a few feet away.

"This is so amazing."

There was an uncomfortable silence. Mickey lay low, close to the wooden deck of the raft. In the darkness they could just make out the shape of each other's heads.

"Well."

"Well." Her voice soared and she giggled, unable to contain her gay excitement.

Alan kicked away from the raft. He took two strokes, then looked back at her. "I'll see you inside, okay?"

"Sure," Mickey answered without thinking.

He waited another moment, his eyes unsuccessfully seeking hers in the dark shadows, before he turned and swam smoothly to the shore.

Mickey watched. What was he doing here? she

wondered. Why was he swimming to her old cottage? Didn't he know? Shouldn't he be going to his family cottage back down the lake?

She could just discern his long, lean, ghostly image as he emerged from the water and ascended her old dock. Then finally he vanished, enveloped by the shroud of darkness. A moment later she saw lights in the cottage switch on.

Diving in, she swam briskly, a vibrant surge of energy propelling her through the cool water. She climbed out of the lake. A thick towel awaited her at the end of the dock. She quickly massaged her scalp, then wrapped the towel around and snug up under her armpits. Gathering her belongings, she ran through the grass to the door and stepped in before she suddenly remembered that this wasn't her home.

Such an eerie feeling. Everything was so familiar and yet so different. In some ways, it felt as if she had never been away, as if they had just returned from an evening of water-skiing. When her towel slipped, she found herself on the verge of giggling with glee. That too was a strangely familiar feeling hidden in the mist of her distant past. This was neither a new place nor home, but it felt like both. Her mind was still reeling from the morning's strange and inexplicable events, and now this peculiar sensation. Tentatively she looked around. Alan was not there. The kitchen light was on, also a table lamp beside the fireplace in the large living room. In the washroom she slipped back into her yellow T-shirt and tan shorts. She slid her fingers through her wet hair; a quick glance in the mirror satisfied her.

Next, another familiar sensation, the unmistakable scent and sizzle of the barbecue. There he was outside on the deck, casually watching the meat cook. For a long while Mickey just stood there transfixed, staring at him through the kitchen window. It was her first chance to see him clearly. This was a man—taller than she had remembered, more robust, his hair darker, much shorter and neater, and his attractive features more precise. Decidedly handsome. He had always been handsome, but in her memories Alan was still a boy, shy and awkward, a friend; the closest thing she had to a brother. Who was he now? she wondered. Still a close friend? An old acquaintance? A stranger?

With determination Mickey bounded back out through the side door, then suddenly she froze. The headlights of a slow-moving car crawled along the dark lane at the back of the cottage. Mickey sank to her knees, cowering behind the wine barrel, peering through the geraniums. The car stopped at the end of the lane. Ready to run, Mickey waited for the sound of doors opening. They didn't. The car jerked forward and slowly continued on its way—two more cottages to the end of the road. Then it stopped again, turned around, and crept back. This time it didn't stop as it slowly passed. Mickey remained outside the door, wondering if it would come back once more. She listened until she could no longer hear the purr of the motor, or the roll of the tires in the still night air.

Her mind raced through possibilities: someone lost, someone looking for a lost dog, for a friend's cottage, someone searching for somebody—who? Her? No, that was impossible. She shuddered. It couldn't be. How could they? Nobody could find her here, it just wasn't possible, and why would they even bother? The unsettling thought was banished from her mind. Deliberately she looked away from the road, resolutely she walked to the front of the cottage.

The moon had begun to rise; the deck was bathed in an iridescent glow. Two lounge chairs were side by side, with only a narrow folding table set between them. On the table there were a bottle of red wine and two long-stemmed glasses. Both glasses were filled.

Walking slowly up behind him, she wrapped her arms around his chest. He shuddered at her touch. She squeezed him snugly. He didn't feel as though he fit quite right somehow.

"Hi," she said simply.

"Hi, I . . ." He tried to twist toward her.

"It is so wonderful to see you." She trembled. Finally she was home, and it was better than she had imagined. Alan was here. She could relax, maybe stay awhile. "It's just so great to see you. I can't believe it." Her grip relaxed, and her arms fell awkwardly to her sides.

"You can't believe it," he scoffed. "What about

me? I swim out to that lonely, empty raft every night, and tonight . . .'' His voice trailed off, and he made one of those shy and whimsical gestures that had always made her giggle like a child.

Alan smiled easily, then looked back at the barbecue. ''I was hungry, thought you might be too,'' he said.

''Absolutely famished.''

''Good.'' He built a hamburger, put it on a plate, and handed it to her. ''If I'd known you were coming, we could have had—''

''No. What could be more perfect than barbecued burgers on the deck? This is perfect.''

Mickey added only barbecue sauce and a thin slice of Spanish onion, then she went to the farthest chair.

''Wine?'' she asked with an approving voice. ''My, my, something has changed. No Rootin-tootin Raspberry?'' She sat down on the comfortable lounge.

''Not even Goofy Grape.'' He smiled. ''You have a good memory. I don't think they even make that stuff anymore.''

''That's a shame.'' Despite not having thought of them in years, she could remember all the weird flavors distinctly, Freckle Face Strawberry, Loopy Lime . . .

''I thought the events were worthy of a wee celebration,'' Alan said. ''Wine.'' He shrugged. ''I know it's not the same as Rootin-tootin Raspberry. I'm sorry.''

"No, wine is perfect."

"Everything is perfect?" he teased her.

"Absolutely," she mumbled through a mouthful of hamburger. Then she couldn't repress another shuddering giggle.

He kept looking at her, then away, then back again, as though he couldn't quite believe his eyes. "I can't believe you are here."

"I am."

"Yes, you are. Slowly it will sink in, it might take me a day or two."

She stretched and luxuriated in the tranquillity. "Listen. It's so quiet. You can here the crickets."

His head nodded slowly. "Hmm, not exactly Malibu, is it? Not terribly exciting."

"It's wonderful," she answered. Quiet, Rootin-tootin Raspberry—did he think she was making fun of him? Fun of the cottage? Fun of this wonderfully peaceful life? Here there was the time and peace to think, to contemplate life, to bask in all life's blessings. "I've really missed this."

Mickey took a slow sip of wine and let it loll about in her mouth before swallowing. Determined to be happy, she immediately perked up. "So, come on, tell me everything," she said with unbridled excitement. "How've you been, what's been happening?"

"Not a whole heck of lot."

"The cottage . . ."

"I bought it." A nervous shrug indicated he wasn't comfortable talking about this.

"I'm glad you did. I'm sure Mom and Dad are too."

"I'm sorry. You know how much I liked your mom and dad."

"I . . ." She felt a potent urge to reach out and touch him. She moved slightly forward. There was an uncomfortable field of force between them, drawing them together but at the same time holding them apart. Every time she came too close she felt its power. It was familiar. It had always been there, for as long as she had known Alan. At times they had been the best of friends, and yet, after not having seen each other in such a very long time, there was still that same feeling of tension, the indecisive need and fear of contact she had felt around Alan when they were both still young teenagers. She had never understood it then. She came from a warm, hugging family—a gregarious blend of Irish and eastern European—you laughed, sang, and shouted, you hugged and kissed all relatives and friends; it was as natural as saying hello when you picked up the telephone.

She desperately wanted to talk but didn't know where to start. There were so many things, and yet she sensed the need to be careful, as though some subjects were tender and perhaps taboo. "Do you live here all the time, Alan?"

"Yes, I got tired of the hassles of living in Toronto.

It's too big, you waste half your life parked in traffic. So I got out.''

"What do you do now?"

He spoke slowly. "I have a modest little business in town.''

She knew he was blushing again. "What?'' she asked gently.

"Promise not to laugh?'' He was grinning now; she knew it without looking.

"Of course I won't laugh,'' Mickey said, already catching her breath.

"Promise?'' He too was already on the verge of laughing.

"Yes. Yes, I promise. What are you, a mortician?'' There was nothing he could possibly say now that wouldn't cause her to burst out laughing.

"Good guess, but no.'' He took a short breath. "Okay, I own the Dairy Duchess in town.''

Her laughter was irrepressible. Her cheeks swelled rosy and her sparkling eyes closed. "That's wonderful,'' Mickey gushed.

"I love it when you laugh.'' Alan shook his head and smiled. "Always laughing. Nobody has a silly laugh like you.''

"Silly!''

"You've got to admit you sound silly, like a . . . seal gasping for breath or something.''

"A seal!''

"Well—''

"I don't. Do I? No!"

"Well—"

"No one has ever said anything like that before," she announced fiercely, but even as she spoke she wondered when was the last time she had been so happy and relaxed, and she let loose with uninhibited laughter. Still she protested, "It's not true."

"Well—"

"Take it back." She made a fist and swung around to threaten him.

He laughed and cowered in fear, closing his eyes and holding up his arms to protect his face. "Okay, okay. But when you really start to laugh," he elaborated hastily, "it's like a very nice, wonderful, pretty little baby seal."

"Baby seal," she scoffed. "What do you know about seals?"

"Well . . ." He grinned as he spoke; there was the old familiar mischievous glint in his soft blue eyes. He continued with mock indignation, "I watch Jacques Cousteau, sometimes." He postured as though that made him an authority on jocular seals.

Mickey shook her head. It almost hurt to let loose and laugh. It had been so long, she was out of practice. Her eyes were wet and her cheeks felt sore.

"So, I'm a baby seal and you are Mr. Dairy Duchess. Alan, that's terrific. So tell me everything. How is business?"

"Pretty good. I also own a little print and copy

shop, and I've got a finger in a couple other little
things. It's fun.''

"A tycoon—"

"That's me, the Donald Trump of Mariposa."

She allowed herself to attempt a little Mae West
imitation, deepening her voice and adding a little
swagger. "Ooh big boy, you know I'm impressed.
Maybe we can do a little business together . . . monkey
business."

Both erupted into laughter. Mickey's laughter was
heightened by embarrassment at her own silliness.

"It sounds so great. We used to go to the Dairy
Duchess all the time. Whenever I'm hot and thirsty, I
remember us nipping into town for a Tempest. Does
that sound good! In fact I craved one today when I
was walking out here. We used to take them down to
Champlain Park, remember, and sit on the wharf talking by the lake."

"I sure do. Let's go." He sat up. "Do you want to
run in for a Tempest?" Alan asked eagerly. "I think
I can get us a bit of a discount."

"Wonderful, I haven't had one in years, since the
last time with you. You know there have actually been
times I've dreamed about them," she said enthusiastically as she sat up. Then she suddenly remembered
the car lights in the back lane, Max squeezing her knee
in the pool, the grim face at the airport. Perhaps she
shouldn't. "But Alan, maybe it would be better another time, okay?" she said, easing back into her

lounge chair. "We've been drinking wine, and well, I'm a little tired and it's so nice right here, right now."

"Yes, it is nice," Alan answered with a tinge of disappointment. "We'll go tomorrow . . . right?"

"For sure."

Alan refilled their glasses.

Mickey took hers and held it between her hands in her lap. "How about your parents?" she asked.

"They're doing fine. They sold our cottage long ago and retired to Florida. I go down once a year during the winter. That's the total extent of my global gallivanting. I'd like to do more, but . . ."

Tied down with business, she concluded. Mickey felt very attracted to Alan, she always had. She felt a yearning to have his long strong arms wrap around her, hug her, comfort her. But he was a friend and somehow she knew it would forever alter the friendship. And a good friend, a trusted friend was something she craved more than anything.

They sat for a while staring out over the water.

"It's been quite a day," Mickey stated simply. They had talked about tomorrow, but Alan hadn't specifically invited her to stay. She knew she could. She knew he expected her to, but she very much wanted to inveigle an explicit invitation to stay the night, just to take some of the bite out of imposing. Around Alan it was as though some of his shyness was infectious and rubbed off on her.

Mickey swallowed the last of her wine. She toyed

with the stem of her empty wineglass, then put it on the table and drank in a deep breath of cool night air.

"You're tired. I'm sorry. We can talk tomorrow." He got up.

"Tired, yes, very. It's been a long day," she said as she stood. "I was in Brazil this morning."

"Brazil?" Alan said, astonished. "This morning? What were you doing there?"

"Leaving as quickly as I could," Mickey stated flatly.

"You are going to tell me all about it, it sounds very exciting."

"It certainly had its moments." Mickey started to gather up the dishes.

"Well," Alan began, "I hope you can stay here for a while." He stood beside her.

"Are you sure it's okay? I'd love to stay for a day or two."

"You know you can stay as long as you want." His voice was dry. "You can have your old room."

For a moment they just hung there very close. Then he reached down and picked up the tray with the wine and the dishes. Mickey went to the barbecue and took the other tray and followed him into the kitchen. The dishes were put into the dishwasher. The leftover wine was put in a cupboard. Then they stood two feet apart and looked at each other.

Mickey was amazed at how awkward she felt. Time had slowed to a crawl. She felt the magnetic attraction of his body drawing her, but an equally strong force held them apart. It seemed impossible to move. She finally broke the spell and stepped toward him.

''Thanks,'' she said.

''For what?''

''For everything, for being here.'' Then she kissed him on the cheek. She parted very slowly, squeezed his forearm in her right hand, and left him standing alone as she vanished into her room. The spell held him suspended there a moment longer.

In the large bedroom, in the front corner of the cottage, diagonally opposite from Mickey's room, Alan rolled over yet again. Sleep was out of the question. He imagined he heard things—footsteps coming toward his room. He sat up in bed and strained to hear. Nothing. He slumped back. But a moment later there it was again. The old floor squeaked. It had to be Mickey. He reached over and snapped on the light. He stood up. Mentally he checked his appearance. He thought about finding a shirt.

The sounds were close, they stopped. Alan took two steps and reached for the door handle.

But the door burst open before he touched it, smacking him on the side of his head with such force that he was sent spinning. Then he was bashed again and he collapsed to the floor.

He awoke groggy, with a splitting headache and a lump the size of a small egg above his right temple.

"Mickey!" he screamed in dismay, the sound of his own voice causing a rush of excruciating pain inside his throbbing skull. Frantically he staggered into her room. She wasn't there. There was nothing, no sign she had ever been there. Had she?

He felt for the swelling on the side of his head. It didn't make sense. In the washroom he found the towel he had left for her on the end of the dock. He touched it. It was still damp. Vividly he remembered every detail of seeing her, every gesture, every feature, every nuance. Of course she had been here. But what had happened? Where was she now? Who had hit him?

In desperation he swung around searching, searching . . . He looked in each room, everywhere he could think of.

Finally, he ran outside. The sun was rising, not even the whisper of a breeze stirred in the trees, the grass was wet with dew. In the backyard—nothing, nothing unusual, another beautiful summer morning. He looked on the deck. He looked under the deck. Nothing. He sprinted to the edge of the water. He stood there staring, looking around. Nothing unusual anywhere.

Taking a deep frustrated breath, he reached down and grabbed a stone and with all his might hurled it out over the water until it kissed the tranquil surface and skipped once, twice, three times, then plop, it sank.

Where could she be? Who bashed his head? She couldn't have done that. Someone else. Who? She was in danger. Kidnapped? Her words echoed in his mind, leaving Brazil, as fast as I can, as fast as I can. Why? It didn't make any sense. What on earth had happened? Reaching down to the stony beach again, he suddenly stopped and looked at a nearby spot on the lawn where the grass wasn't the normal thick and dark green. Instead there was a distinct patch of bare earth and sprouts of sickly white and bright yellow—light starved grass that had been hidden from the sun.

The little yellow sailboat was gone.

Chapter Two

With cupped hands Mickey reached forward as far as she could manage, grabbed at the water, pulled, and thrust it behind her. The little sailboat responded with a shimmy and reluctantly wiggled forward a few feet, barely causing a ripple in the smooth mirrorlike surface. She did it again, and again . . . and again, as she had all night. Over and over with a steady rhythm. Her arms ached, her back ached, but she refused to acknowledge the gnawing pain. Instead she continued to propel the little craft onward. Shortly after sunrise she neared a low and sandy shoreline. Exhausted, her back and shoulders throbbing, she elected to wade the last few feet knee-deep in the cool water, trailing the boat behind. Being able to straighten her back and stretch her legs provided a respite of sweet agony.

The area was rampant with frolicking children—a summer camp in full peak-season chaos. The children backed away as she dragged the boat up onto the beach. She lifted her arms to the sun, groaned, twisted her spine back and forth, stretching out her cramped and aching muscles.

A tall, gangly teenager with a black plastic whistle around his neck confronted her, but before he could speak Mickey interjected, "I claim this heathen land in the name of King George the Third! Long live the king." She didn't smile. It was meant to be a joke, but she didn't have the energy or the enthusiasm to muster a smile. She slung her pack over her shoulder, left the boat, and kept going. "I hope you don't mind," she added as she brushed past the startled boy. He merely fell back a step and gawked.

She walked right through the camp, between the log cabins, among motley tribes of junior white-skinned Indian braves decked out with head feathers and messy war paint, and across the left field of a baseball game, all the way out to a gravel road that led her to the highway. First she looked south, in the direction of Mariposa, the cottage, and Alan. Hesitating for a moment, she considered returning. Maybe that would confuse her pursuers. Maybe she should just stand up to them anyway. What could they do? The situation was becoming more absurd all the time.

Then she remembered Lorenzo's black, brooding eyes—he was capable of anything, and whereas

Lorenzo was sinister and calculating, Sam was flip and wild. Lorenzo would hurt someone because he had to—neither reluctantly nor eagerly, but Sam enjoyed and cultivated his own personal streak of viciousness. They were fierce and unpredictable; Mickey never wanted to risk meeting either of them again. And she certainly didn't want to cause Alan any more trouble.

Her heart seemed to stutter when she thought of abandoning Alan the way she had. What would he think when he woke up and she was gone? She'd call first chance she got and try to explain. Clearly, her only choice now was to put as much distance as quickly as she could between herself and Sam and Lorenzo. That meant leaving wonderful Mariposa, and wonderful Alan behind. Mickey chewed at the inside of her cheek to stop from crying. Clearly it wasn't a choice she enjoyed.

With resignation she crossed the road and started walking north along the narrow, winding highway.

It was hot again. The air was so thin and dry it hurt to breathe. Today she would thumb a ride as soon as she could. She wanted to get far away, quickly, the farther the better. Maybe in Vancouver she could relax and think.

With the sound of each approaching car she paused, studiously inspecting the moving vehicle, then tentatively held out an upturned thumb. She had an idea what sort of vehicle Lorenzo and Sam might have. She guessed it was the slow-moving car she had seen prowling the lane behind the cottage. It was dark, so she hadn't seen it well, but it seemed fairly large, and she surmised it would be a rental car, so it would be clean and modern. The seventh car pulled over just ahead and waited on the shoulder.

Mickey jogged the few yards to where a large old gold sedan had coasted to a stop. Rust had eaten through corners of the fenders and at the base of the door. Inside the car was clean but the upholstery was threadbare. The front seat had a brown, fuzzy-looking slipcover. She sized the driver up carefully: a young man, scant of hair, with a gentle face and a wide, gap-tooth smile: He was big and soft-looking, like a friendly teddy bear; he wore faded navy blue coveralls with an embroidered name tag, JOHNIE.

Mickey opened the door. ''Thanks. Where are you going?''

''Where you headed?'' he responded.

''Come now, I asked you first.'' Mickey smiled as she slipped in through the passenger door.

''I'm going to Sandhurst,'' he said finally.

''Great, me too.''

After a quick nod he glanced at his sideview mirror, then waited for a car to pass before pulling back out onto the highway. ''Do you know someone there?'' he asked.

''No. It just sounds like a nice place,'' Mickey answered, not even certain where it was.

''Nice little town, I guess. Not much doing, perks

up in summer a bit, what with the provincial park nearby, cottagers and whatnot. You staying at the park, or with friends, or what?''

Mickey took a long deep breath. As the car accelerated she glanced back over her shoulder. For a while the driver worked on establishing a friendly banter. Mickey tried to cooperate but her heart wasn't in it. Gradually they both gave up. She slumped down into her seat and leaned against the door. She kept struggling with tears and that annoyed her. *I should be relieved, Max will never find me now. It can't be worth his effort.* She remembered having reached that erroneous conclusion before. But that had nothing to do with those tears that dampened her eyes. At first she didn't understand. Then, like a huge weight settling down upon her shoulders that she gradually accepted, the truth came to her—*I found a chance for happiness, and now I'm fleeing from it.*

Her eyes closed and she managed a short rest before the driver tapped her on the shoulder. They were stopped beside a gas station at one end of the meager main street of Sandhurst.

''This is it. This is as far as I go. I work here,'' he said.

Thanking Johnie, she struggled to get out, then stood weary and confused. She was eager to be on her way but her stomach was growling in protest. With her future uncertain, it was hard to know when she would have another opportunity to grab some food.

The row of little stores called out and her stomach responded with enthusiasm.

The town was old and hadn't changed much for fifty years. There was a string of motley storefronts, mostly red brick with dingy windows and faded signs. Mickey crossed the intersection, dawdled in front of a bakery, and drank in the sweet, yeasty fragrance. She stared in the window admiring the big sticky Chelsea buns especially, but upon calculating her finances—she had a few American dollars, but her credit card was nearly at its limit thanks to her rush flight from São Paulo— she continued reluctantly down the street past the red-and-gold sign of a Chinese food restaurant, and a video store.

A little bell rang as she pushed open the door to a small grocery store. The rickety shelves were crammed, the hardwood floors creaked, the place smelled musty.

She knew it was more than a thousand miles to the next major city, Winnipeg—that was the direction she had decided to go—and about three thousand miles to Vancouver, and she wasn't sure exactly how best to get there, but she knew it would be wise to conserve money and prepare for the worst. Picking up only a loaf of whole wheat bread, a small jar of peanut butter, and a one-liter jar of apple juice—she figured she could reuse the jar as a canteen, refilling it with water from time to time—Mickey headed to the cashier. Not a very exciting breakfast, but these three items could be stretched into a number of meals, she thought.

Her hands were occupied with the task of carrying the groceries and the knapsack, so she used her backside to push open the glass door to leave. Stopping in the doorway, she noticed a pay phone on the wall. She turned back. Using her calling card, she got Alan's number from the operator and dialed. It rang eleven times with no answer. She tried the Dairy Duchess. As she counted out the rings, she stared at the phone and glanced down at her feet, then out the front window to the street and caught a glimpse of the gas station. There was a small blue sedan, new, a Cavalier— could be a rental car, she speculated, and it wasn't at the pumps getting gas. The driver had parked near the office door. Two men were talking; one was the young fellow, Johnie, who had given her the ride. He was pointing and gesturing, and all she could see of the other man was the shadow of his back.

A rush of fear consumed her. She was too tired to think. Where could she hide? The town was small. There was only the main street, which forked off the highway for a few hundred yards, then merged again, plus a few houses and a couple of gravel side roads that wandered into the bush enroute to nearby lakes and summer cottages. Out on the roads or the highway she'd be found before she could catch a ride; she might last longer hiding in the stores but sooner or later they'd find her.

*   *   *

Down the street Johnie pointed to the spot where he had dropped off the pretty girl with the golden skin and the wild copper hair.

"Ten minutes ago?" Alan repeated.

"Well, no more than fifteen."

"Where'd she go?"

"At first nowheres," Johnie answered. "I mean, I started opening up and all, and I kept seeing her standing there, sort of confused like, then I was going to go say something, see if I could help her, you know, and then, there she was, gone."

Excitedly Alan thanked the man and quickly got back into his car. Obviously, she was running from something, or someone, and trying to hide. No doubt, that's why she had come to Mariposa in the first place. She could be anywhere, he thought. There is so much empty space up here, miles of nothing; it's an ideal place to disappear. Would she go to the provincial park? Did she know someone else nearby? Most likely she went back out to the highway and grabbed another ride. He spun the car around in a circle and headed toward the highway.

On hands and knees Mickey crept forward. The black tar roof was glowing warm in the sun. She raised her head cautiously. Over the short brick wall at the storefront, she could see the garage. The blue Cavalier was gone. It wasn't on the main street either, at least not on the sections she could see, and she could see most of it. Sinking back down onto the flat roof, she felt a rush of relief and then a bitter spark of sadness. How had it come to this? A car stops at a gas station and she is reduced to scurrying up fire escapes, hiding on roofs. What's next, jumping into garbage Dumpsters? The car could have been there for any number of reasons. She couldn't hide every time she saw a car, or a person; jump every time she heard a noise! But what else could she do? Every passing car, every stranger, every noise behind her—how could she be sure they weren't Sam or Lorenzo?

Taking another quick peek, she realized a large white Chrysler, also shining clean and new, had stopped at the service station almost exactly where the Cavalier had been—obviously, stopping at a gas station for directions is a very common practice. She collapsed back onto the warm black tar paper roof. Mickey felt content to lay there baking in the warm sun, if not forever, at least for a little while longer. She opened her jar of apple juice and took a drink.

Inside her raged confusion. If only she had never met Max. Her life would be still normal. She calculated the date; in fact, if all had gone according to plan tomorrow was the day she should have been returning to Los Angeles. She'd be back in her little apartment. The thought was only superficially calming; the truth was she wasn't terribly happy in huge and impersonal L.A. Perhaps it would be different if she had grown up there. Maybe with time, she pondered, maybe if she met someone it would be different. Maybe it would be wise not to go back there, maybe she should think of starting fresh somewhere new, or somewhere . . . She chided herself. Maybe I should never have met Max, it was too late. Somehow, I should figure out how to lose Sam and Lorenzo permanently.

She opened the jar of peanut butter and used her finger as a knife. After eating a surprisingly delicious sandwich, she lay back and dozed.

Had someone shouted her name? That's what it sounded like. She was dreaming, she had to be. Opening her eyes, she attempted to hear better.

"Mickey . . . Mickey!" Loud and insistent, someone was indeed calling her name—who? It sounded like . . .

Cautiously she lifted her head. There he was, Alan, stationary on the white line in the middle of the main street; he was standing in one spot, but pivoting in a circle and patiently scanning the village. A car passed slowly behind him. The driver stared. Several people had stopped on the sidewalks and stared. Then Alan took a deep breath and screamed like a lunatic, "Mickey . . . Mickey!" He waited, searching the sidewalks and storefronts, then shrugged and began to leave.

Mickey shot to her feet. "Alan," she called and waved with both arms.

He spun around.

"Up here."

It took a moment for him to look above the rows of people on the street up to the blue sky—there she was among the wisps of white cloud. Their eyes met and he leaped up with joy, hands high in victory.

In the alley at the bottom of the fire escape, she fell into his arms and hugged him, snuggling deep into his welcoming chest, not knowing whether to laugh or cry, and he hugged her in return until he tensed and broke apart from her.

"Mickey, what the heck is going on?"

They were at the mouth of the alley. Dozens of people now filled the sidewalks, or stood holding open shop doors, murmuring to latecomers about the young stranger who had stood in the middle of town and screamed, and the girl who had popped up on the roof of the Red and White grocery store. Crazy summer cottagers—that was the consensus the townsfolk arrived at, playing some fool game of hide-and-seek or something.

Aware of the little swirl of sensation they had created, Mickey pulled at his hand. "Come on, let's get out of here," she implored.

Alan barely moved. "Are you okay?"

"I'm okay." She yanked on his arm. "But let's go."

Still he didn't succumb to her insistent tugging. "Okay, let's find the nearest police station."

"What will we tell the police?" she asked, beginning to move.

"Well . . ." He was lost for words.

"Alan, we should just get out of here. Can we, Alan? You can just drop me somewhere different."

"I . . ." Perplexed, he looked about, as though seeking help with an answer. Myriad blank faces stared back at him.

"Please," she said. "Come on, I'll explain everything."

Reluctantly Alan led her to his car. He didn't move quickly. He was still unsure, confused.

"But why are they chasing you?" he asked as he opened the door.

"It's not what you think," she said over the top of the car.

"I don't think anything. I don't know what to think." Bending over, he slid into the driver's seat, then unlocked her door.

Mickey tossed her knapsack in the back and jumped in beside him. It appeared the entire population of the small town plus many local cottagers doing their shopping now lined the sidewalks waiting to watch a parade. If anyone came by searching for her, every soul would remember.

"I'll tell you everything," she said, "but please, we have to get away from here, fast."

"Okay, okay," he repeated as though trying to convince himself this truly was the right thing to do. "Which way?"

"North . . . no! Start like you are going south, then out at the highway we'll turn and go north."

Alan's eyes questioned her.

"Just in case," she answered.

He drove south down the main street to the highway and waited at the stop sign for a string of several cars to pass by. In the vast wilderness of Northern Ontario there was only one narrow, two-lane highway, a thin ribbon of asphalt around which almost all civilization was strung like a few tiny beads on a very long string. They could take the road south, the way they had come into town, or north to even fewer beads and greater desolation.

"Thanks," Mickey said softly as the car surged forward. "I'm so very sorry about getting you into all this."

Alan shifted gears; he didn't respond.

"I'm sorry about last night. I snuck out of there when I heard people by the house. It's me they want— I never dreamed they were going to hurt you," she said gingerly, drawing the hair aside to examine the black-purple swelling above his temple.

"It's okay."

"And I took your sailboat."

"I know. Don't worry about it. It was your old boat anyway. Just tell me, what is going on?"

Mickey answered simply, "Two men are chasing me."

"Why?"

"I don't know why."

Her answer made him flinch and glance upon her.

"I mean, I have an idea, but it sounds sort of . . . silly. I'm really not sure what is going on."

"If someone is chasing you, why can't we go to the police?" Then his voice changed, becoming gentler. "Did you do anything wrong?"

"What do you mean?"

"Commit a crime?"

"No," she answered without hesitating or flinching.

He never doubted her. "Then why not go to the police? Tell them."

"Tell them what?" Mickey asked.

"That these goons have been trying to get you."

Mickey was quiet. "Because I don't see how the police could help. What would they do, guard me? And it's all so crazy. I keep thinking they have to give up and go home. I keep thinking I've lost them, then there they are again. They just keep coming. And I don't know what they are trying to do. Or why they bother. Why are they going to all this trouble?"

He was driving quickly. They were already long out of town. The countryside was all protruding lumps of pink granite, fir trees, scrub brush, and scattered lakes sparkling in the sun. Northern Ontario is much larger than the state of Texas, and for hundreds of thousands of square miles, on either side of the highway and the one lonely rail line that links Canada together, that's almost all there is, the low undulating rock of the Ca-

nadian Shield, wild rugged bush, and tens of thousands
of scattered pools of water.

"Come back to Mariposa."

"I can't."

"Why?"

"They'll find me there." *They'll cause you trouble,*
she added to herself.

"What then?" Alan asked.

"I'll just disappear for a while. They won't be able
to find me."

"*I* found you."

"I know." As she thought about it her eyes wid-
ened with amazement. "How? How'd you find me?"

He answered with a grin, "You are the one of those
people everyone notices." He pulled out to pass a
large, ponderous motor home. "I discovered the sunfish was missing, figured you must have slipped out
in it last night when your friends arrived. . . ."

"My friends!"

"Well, whoever they are. Then I got my ski boat
out from the marina and drove around the lake looking
for the sunfish. I found it at that kid's summer camp
and started asking everyone if they had seen you. Of
course everyone had. A counselor said you walked out
to the highway and started hitchhiking north. I zipped
back home, got the car, and raced after you. I stopped
everywhere. A guy at a gas station said he had given
you a lift. Blind luck. In fact I almost lost you. I decided you'd come back out to the highway looking for

another ride, so I looked there but didn't see you. I figured you probably had already caught a ride, but I wanted to bc sure you weren't still in town, so I decided to . . ." He shrugged. It wasn't necessary to tell the rest.

"You're brilliant."

"Right," he scoffed, "except at the moment I can't figure out what is going on."

"They'll give up." They should have given up already. "Even if they don't, they won't be able to find me."

"Mickey, they found you at the cottage. They seem pretty good at finding you. How'd they know you were at the cottage?"

"I guess I talked a lot about the place, and when I flew to Toronto instead of L.A., I saw Sam board the plane at the last second in São Paulo. I gave him the slip at customs in Toronto. Somehow he followed me to Mariposa. He just guessed right. He is sort of trained to do this kind of stuff . . . and worse, I'm afraid. Then he must have met up with Lorenzo. I hadn't seen Lorenzo on the flight, but I'm pretty sure I saw him last night."

"So who are they?"

Mickey hesitated. It wasn't that she didn't want to tell Alan, it was just that she really didn't understand herself what was going on, or how to explain it clearly. "It's no big deal, really."

"Chasing you thousands of miles is no big deal?"

Mickey looked studiously through the window at the passing bush, then she looked back at Alan. He continued to watch the highway, but she knew he could also see her. He was waiting.

She swiveled sideways on her seat, tugging out some slack from the seat belt, and watched him carefully as she spoke. She decided to start at the very beginning with the move to Los Angeles, which she hadn't liked, but it was a great career opportunity for her father, so she never complained. She finished university and had just taken a teaching job when her mother died after a long illness. It was hard on her father; they were so very close, and he died suddenly and unexpectedly. Her sister had already moved to Vancouver, where she'd married and was working in public relations with a large bank.

So that left Mickey alone in Los Angeles, a schoolteacher, which she enjoyed, but all in all not very settled. She just didn't feel like she fit in with the West Coast mentality. She didn't care much for fancy cars, or expensive clothes; she preferred burgers to heart of palm and sushi. She was ready for a change, or at least a little break.

It was summer holidays, and a teacher friend, Samantha Edwards, someone she didn't know too well, but who taught at the same school, asked her to go along on a trip to Latin America: four stops, the Yucatán Peninsula of Mexico to see the Mayan ruins, Rio de Janeiro, Buenos Aires, and then the Inca ruins at Machu Picchu. It was going to be expensive, but history was her pet passion, it sounded exciting, and she wanted to get away for a while so she went. It was actually Samantha who first befriended Max Baerga at a nightclub in their hotel. That resulted in a visit to his luxurious villa. Somehow Max decided he was in love with Mickey, and Samantha discreetly vanished.

"She probably thought she was doing me a favor by disappearing," Mickey added with a shrug.

Alan interrupted. "In love with you?" he repeated, trying to get a grip on the ramifications.

"Well, it seems like. It's hard to explain. He actually treated me with great respect. He even gave me presents." Mickey held her right hand forward near the dash. "Like this ring. I'd forgotten all about it."

"Looks pretty expensive."

"I guess, but I certainly don't want it. I didn't want it when he gave it to me. He insisted. I was going to leave it behind when I left, or send it back to him. It was all so hectic, I forgot. Now, I don't know. I can't exactly throw it away." She looked at the ring. The disgust in her eyes abruptly vanished. "I'm going to donate it to some charity," she said, then added with sudden inspiration, "one that works with underprivileged children in the third world."

"Mickey, I still don't understand. So this guy was in love with you. . . ." He left the thought dangling for her to pick up and carry on.

"I certainly don't understand either. I mean, I made it clear I wasn't interested."

"Why didn't you just leave?"

"I tried. A couple of times, but I was frightened of getting Max angry, of provoking a confrontation. Sam, and this other guy, Lorenzo—Lorenzo especially made it seem like if push came to shove they'd force me to stay."

"Because he was in love with you?"

"Yes, but more because he was accustomed to getting his own way. Max was incredibly rich, and handsome, and he could really turn on the charm, when he wanted to, and when that didn't work he would use force. I saw the way he dealt with people. People were in awe of him, terrified." She took a labored breath and shuddered a little as she exhaled. "At first I sort of even liked the guy. It was kind of exciting." She shook her head. "I just wasn't thinking straight."

Mickey looked away, then back. "I knew it was all wrong. Max was wrong. At first I didn't really know him at all, not the real him. I couldn't stand it, the overwhelming luxury amid such abject poverty." She shuddered again. "And Max, well, Max had another side. He had great wealth, and in Brazil that means great power, absolute power. He was like a god. He ordered people around like cattle, or pushed them about like chess pieces. He didn't care. He always got what he wanted, always, everything. Yes, I tried to leave and he wouldn't let me. Maybe I didn't try hard enough—he intimidated me, scared me. People were only allowed to do what Max told them. So, instead of telling him I was leaving I just slipped out when no one was watching, and believe me, that wasn't as easy as it sounds.''

Alan waited for a second, expecting her to continue. He didn't want to rush her. ''And?'' he finally had to prompt.

''And I came here.''

''And?'' Alan asked.

''And what?''

''And that's it?'' he said with surprise. ''You ran away. That's all, and this guy is trying to get you back?''

''Seems like,'' Mickey answered.

''That's . . .'' Alan tried to comprehend what she had said.

''Hard to believe?'' Mickey suggested.

''He send some thugs after you, just because you left him?''

''Yes . . . no. Maybe because it looks bad on him. Maybe he thinks it sets a bad precedent if people just stop following orders, then his businesses—which I don't know, but I don't think were legitimate—would be in trouble. It's all I can come up with, I don't know.''

Alan's eyes slipped off the road and sought out hers, finally succeeding. His gentle eyes caught and held her. His hand caught and held her hand. His eyes skipped away to the road and when he looked back, Mickey's eyes had wandered off to gaze blankly into the blur of green trees. Alan still held her hand, and gave it a squeeze; she glanced back at him, eyes now moist.

"You didn't do anything wrong, Mickey. Don't worry, we can handle this."

She tried but failed to return his smile.

He continued, "And I think it's resulted in some real good luck, anyway." He grinned. "Serendipity."

"What?"

"Serendipity—doesn't that mean accidental good fortune?"

"What good fortune?"

"Well," he began slowly, "you're here. And despite everything I can't remember the last time I was this happy."

This time she did succeed in smiling. When she dug down through her physical exhaustion, the mental confusion and fear, the anxiety over what to do next, and where were Sam and Lorenzo, and could they possibly find her again—if she could push that all aside, then yes, deep in her heart she had a small warm glow of happiness, and it crept in through the firm, gentle hand that held hers snug in its grasp.

"Yeah? You know, I'm sort of happy too."

The strong comfort of his hand gave her confidence.

A warm and cozy mile ticked by before Alan asked in his gentle voice, "Now what?"

Immediately the turmoil swept back into her heart. Now what? To her the choice was between what she wanted to do and what she should do. She said simply, "I'll head out west."

Alan responded. "Okay, I'll drive you."

"No, I couldn't impose like that."

"It's a gorgeous day for a drive."

"No, I mean to Winnipeg, probably to Vancouver."

"Sounds great. I've always wanted to drive across our great country."

"Alan, it'll take almost a week."

"Terrific. Sounds better and better all the time."

"Alan, you can't. What about your businesses?"

"I'm the boss. I just get in the way, ask anyone."

"I don't believe that."

He smiled, staring straight ahead out through the windshield, then he spoke slowly, painfully, choosing his words with care. "You know," he faltered but continued with steely determination, and a faint spark of joy, "when we were kids, all those times I'd tell you I was going out to Yorkdale or downtown, or up to the cottage or . . . wherever, that it wasn't out of my way, and I could give you a lift, if you wanted. Well, I usually wasn't planning to go to any of those places, and it was out of my way, but I didn't mind, I just wanted to spend some time with you. Then one winter you vanished and each summer I'd come by your cottage and it would be closed up, and I kept hoping you and your family would return for the summer at least one more time. Of course, I knew you were in Los Angeles, but when you left, your parents didn't know for how long it would be. And I know they planned to come back in the summers occasionally. But I guess they got too busy. Then finally it went up for sale, and I thought, she isn't coming back. I'm never going to see her again, not even as a friend. I thought about finding you and calling you and maybe flying down for a little visit, I thought about all sorts of crazy things, but . . .'' He shrugged and stared ahead out the windshield. "Then, like a miracle, you suddenly appear after all these years . . .''

"Alan . . .'' Mickey couldn't think of what to say. She wanted to touch him, her body ached for a good warm hug, but she couldn't. Even if they weren't hurtling down the highway she wouldn't have been able to. That strange, invisible barrier was back and more powerful than ever—the intense need of contact and the fear of it. It made her shudder. She squeezed his hand; he squeezed back but shortly after drew his hand away.

Alan flipped on the turn signal and pulled out to pass a lumber truck. He accelerated sharply. Several cars followed in a snaking line behind, all swerving out to pass the slow-moving truck. There was a fairly steady flow of summer traffic on the highway— vacationers mostly, some with tent trailers in tow, or canoes on the roof, enough traffic of varying speed to make traveling on a hilly, winding, two-lane highway a challenge.

A few minutes of easy silence passed before Alan resurfaced from his thoughts. He spoke slowly. "What are these guys going to do if they catch you, take you back? They can't take you back. Are you sure there isn't something more to it?"

Mickey answered in a hushed and pensive voice, "I don't know. And I don't intend to find out."

"Well, they are nowhere near here," Alan announced with confidence. "Even if they asked around and found out you'd been in Sandhurst and knew we went back to the highway, even if they knew we went north instead of south, they'd have to stop and ask a lot of people if they'd seen us, and we've been driving straight, stopping only for gas. At best, or I should say, at worst, they still must be way behind."

"Sounds great."

"Maybe they've finally given up and, right this instant, they're winging their way back to South America."

"Most likely," Mickey concurred with a cheerful smile and nod. "I mean, what were they going to do if they caught me anyway, drag me back kicking and screaming to São Paulo?"

"It's crazy."

"Crazy."

"Absurd."

"Absolutely."

"But let's keep going, just in case."

"Yes, we should keep going, just in case."

The sun set. There was a short explosion of vibrant colors on the horizon ahead, then darkness quickly descended. They drove on into the night. Soon there were fewer piercing headlights racing across the black barren wilderness. Hours passed.

Mickey watched Alan in the darkness. He seemed to be far away, deep in his own meditative reverie. What had he said? "I just wanted to be with you." She considered that but that girl, that Mickey, was only a memory now. They were friends, that much she was sure of. She felt they would always be friends, even if thirty years slipped by without their seeing each other, they would still be forever friends. And that was a nice warm feeling.

Mickey's eyes flickered closed. She shook her head to spring them open, but moments later her eyes would close again. Her head would sag low, then kick up, and she would be awake, bleary eyed and with a crick in her neck but awake once more, only to stare blankly ahead, before her eyelids would feel heavy and droop down and she'd begin the routine once more.

"Why don't you sleep in the back?" Alan suggested again. He'd suggested it several times before.

"No. I want to keep you company."

"Come on, you're exhausted."

"You must be too," she rejoined.

"I'm okay."

Mickey thought for a second. She did crave a chance to close her eyes, grab a short, refreshing nap. Her entire body ached with fatigue; she hadn't slept since the little snooze on the swimming raft—when had that been?—yet she couldn't leave Alan. He was tired as well. He shouldn't be driving alone. "Let's stop somewhere, just pull off onto one of these little dirt side roads and catch an hour's sleep before the sun rises."

Alan contemplated the suggestion. "Of course, nobody could possibly find us. It'll be okay."

Slowing down the car, he watched for a chance to turn. He took the first opportunity he came upon. Just as they cleared off of the highway and onto the dirt path, there was a flash and a large white car whipped along the highway behind them.

Slowly Alan followed the rough dirt trail for twenty yards and stopped the car beneath a fragrant pine, facing a small lake. They could just see it glinting silver in the moonlight.

"If I had any energy left I'd go for a swim," Mickey said. "I feel so grimy. Maybe in the morning." Already she was climbing into the backseat and stretching out. She used her knapsack as a pillow, which she wrestled with, trying to get it soft and comfortable before she gave up and just lay still. Surprisingly, sleep didn't come quickly. Tired, but tense, her mind wouldn't shut down.

"Alan?" she whispered.

"Yes," he answered.

"Are you okay? Have you got enough room?"

"Yes." He had cranked back the bucket seat and it lay inches above her knees. She could see his face in the moonlight, and that made her feel good.

It was very quiet. Only the endless chatter of frogs and insects disrupted the tranquility. The air was brilliantly crisp and fresh. Already there was a faint gray glow spreading out from low on the eastern horizon.

Alan spoke softly. "Are you still awake?"

"Yes."

"Are you okay?"

"I'm fine," she answered. Then she continued, "It's funny, I just can't sleep right now. I can't relax."

A moment later she had fallen into a deep sleep.

Chapter Three

After a sharp click, there was silence, then, close by her head, another sound; a long creak and a dull crack, precisely the sound a car door makes when it is opened slowly.

Mickey stirred but fought off the impulse to wake. Whatever it was it would go away; she was too tired, too wrapped in the dry cobwebs of a deep sleep. Nonetheless, from somewhere inside there percolated an unusual sense of urgency. She tried to pry open her eyes. They opened a sliver, then quivered and closed tight. Through that sliver, for the instant they'd been open, she had seen a dark figure blocking the sunlight. Still she was quite content to slide back into slumber. When a large hand descended upon the top of her head and shook her, she fought once more to pry open her eyes.

Through fluttering squints she discovered Sam towering over her. Still feeling dreamy, at first not remembering where she was or who he was, still breathing deep and slow, she blinked and focused and contemplated. Then she jerked bolt upright.

In the east, the sun, as large and orange as a basketball, was clearly visible. Its bright golden beams filtered through a grand porous barrier of pine and spindly white birch trees. A chorus of contented birds accompanied by the occasional burst of excited prattle from a squirrel and the constant bleats of frogs created an intriguing and joyous natural symphony. Every few moments the music was underscored by the whistle of a car or a truck thundering down the highway.

In the backseat Alan and Mickey sat side by side waiting like chastened schoolchildren outside a principal's office. Lorenzo and Sam stood nonchalantly leaning up against the rear fender of Alan's car, speaking in Portuguese. Sam held an open map and did most of the talking. Animated, he laughed and pointed as if he was relating a humorous story to friends. Lorenzo barely moved. Only when Mickey started to whisper did Lorenzo whirl around and pay his prisoners any heed. "Shut up," he commanded in a fierce voice, and for a moment even the wildlife acquiesced.

Compared with Mickey, Alan was surprisingly calm, as though now with everyone present the situation could be resolved. Mickey was more agitated than ever. Twice she tried to communicate surreptitiously with Alan. She tried again, whispering, ''We've got to get away.''

Immediately she incurred the wrath of Lorenzo. He smashed the revolver butt hard against the window. The glass shattered into a tumult of uniform chunks that rained down onto her lap like loose kernels of frozen corn. The swift, volatile reaction caused her body to contract in a violent spasm. She shook and then turned into Alan's waiting arms.

Lorenzo dispassionately lowered the pistol through the missing window. He aimed directly at her. She glared back at him, trying not to look afraid. He pulled the trigger. He let the gun kick slightly up and to the side. Terror jolted Mickey up out of her seat. The cannonading blast threatened to burst her eardrums, but the bullet missed. Instead it punched through the opposite window leaving a small round hole and a spider web of cracked glass. Lorenzo held the revolver there before her eyes, close, so close Mickey had to refocus to see it.

''Please, don't talk,'' he said in a calm and mockingly kind voice. She stared at the black steel barrel, the drum, the hammer. ''Understand?'' he asked, but he didn't wait for an answer.

Mickey nodded. The gun was gone.

Sam was grinning from ear to ear. He was enjoying himself.

* * *

The violent eruption still ricocheted in her ears and reverberated up and down her spine all the way to a sharp tingle in her fingers and toes. Another truck lumbered by out on the highway. She began to wonder if someone may have heard the shot. The highway was close, but not close enough.

With casual impunity Lorenzo turned his back to them and lit a cigarette with a gold lighter. A thin gold bracelet dangled from his scrawny wrist. He barked a few words in Portuguese. Sam responded with an agreeable nod and lit his own cigarette from the gold lighter.

Alan was breathing hard but evenly. It was his first opportunity to really observe them. They dressed similarly—expensive lightweight, pale linen suits but no dress shirt or tie. Instead they each wore polo shirts; Lorenzo's was black and Sam's purple. Their eyes were hidden behind dark wraparound sunglasses. But other than that, they looked entirely different.

Lorenzo's skin was dark and reddish like ground cinnamon. Slim, short, and wiry, every move or even slight shift he made was quick and fluid with catlike grace. Lorenzo exuded an elegant, unpredictable, and terrifying élan.

Sam, on the other hand, possessed a dull, sluggish power. Tall, with a pasty face, an oxlike barrel chest, and big chubby hands, he was no less menacing. He spoke with the trace of an English accent. Despite spending most of his life in Brazil he had not adapted to the heat and humidity of the Canadian summer heat wave; he was perspiring like an ice cube in the sun.

Lorenzo spoke again. Mickey cocked her head to listen. Then she turned to watch him walk back out to the highway.

Sam came to the shattered rear window of Alan's car. "Fun time," he announced. Then he said to Alan, brandishing his pistol for emphasis, "Now then, how 'bout you hop up into the front."

Alan hesitated for a moment before starting to open the rear door. Sam kicked the door back shut with his foot. Using his pistol barrel as a pointer he indicated that Alan was to climb over the seat. He did. Next Sam opened the back door and pointed the gun at Mickey. He winked at her and waggled the gun back and forth to indicate he wanted her in the front as well, in the driver's seat. When she was there he got into the back, brushing away some of the nuggets of broken glass.

Driving into view came a large white Chrysler. Sam instructed, "Tag along behind, shall we." Then he added in a smug voice, "We're going for a little jaunt in the country."

Lorenzo passed by and continued along the dirt road. He was headed away from the highway.

Mickey pulled the seat belt around her waist and snapped it in place. Alan did the same. The key was still in the ignition. She turned it. The motor started and she pumped the gas a little. Then she fiddled with the mirror until she was satisfied; next, she started to adjust the seat, jerking it forward, then easing it back. She was stalling, trying to gain time, time to think.

"Come now, dear, hurry along," Sam said impatiently.

Putting the car in gear, Mickey let out the clutch and started to follow Lorenzo. One side at a time, Sam reached forward and pushed down the lock buttons for the front doors. He sat in the middle of the backseat. His full-moon face filled Mickey's rearview mirror.

"Where are we going?" Alan demanded.

"For a little ride. Maybe we'll find a nice spot and have a picnic. Go swimming. That'll be fun, won't it?"

"This is crazy," Alan said.

Sam continued, "Come now, I know you like swimming, Mickey."

Swimming? Mickey looked ahead. She was trying to devise an plan of escape, but her thoughts kept leaping away. Plenty of nice places for a picnic, plenty of nice places to go swimming, he was just taunting them. She knew what they were planning. There wasn't time to waste thinking of anything but escape.

"What is it you want?" Alan asked.

"Mickey knows," Sam answered. "Don't you, Mickey, dear?"

She was tense, concentrating. She almost didn't hear him. Then she spat out her answer. "I don't know. I have no idea why you are doing this."

Sam laughed. "Of course you do," he replied happily.

"I think this is absolutely crazy," Alan protested.

"Perhaps," Sam said casually, "but who cares what you think?"

Mickey resolved to say nothing. Instead, she tried to concentrate on what she was doing. It had been awhile since she had driven a car with a standard transmission. She rotated the steering wheel back and forth, trying to get the feel of the steering mechanism. She shifted gears. Nervously she tapped the breaks and goosed the gas just a little. Driving skills were critical; she wanted to be ready.

"What's the point?" Alan continued. "You can't just demand . . ."

"Shut up," Sam commanded.

"You won't get away with this. Not here."

The barrel of the pistol tapped Alan sharply on the side of the head. "Shut up," Sam said once more.

Alan grabbed at the gun but Sam had anticipated the action and jerked the gun away. "Listen," he said, snarling, "sit still and shut up or I'll kill you right now."

"He will," Mickey said, her voice screeching with the tension. "He will."

Settling back into the seat, Sam smirked. "Yes, of course, I will. I will," he repeated with glee.

Lorenzo headed deeper and deeper into the bush. The roads were only sandy paths sliced through the

forest to enable the loggers to get in and get the lumber
out. The area they traversed had been logged out many
years before. It was erratically rolling country, a confused mix of naked rock and scrub brush, frequently
interrupted with a tangled assortment of lake and
pond, river and marsh.

The car in front threw up a blizzard of gritty sand.
Alan's car didn't have air-conditioning and it was too
hot to close all the windows, even if they still could.
Mickey let Lorenzo get well ahead, so she could see
better and stop the dust from streaming in. Sam didn't
complain. He sat quietly in the back with his gun in
his hand, grinning happily, intently watching them
both. Gradually Lorenzo got still farther off in front.

Mickey cleared her throat. She gave Alan an anxious look, and with her right hand low on the seat,
where Sam couldn't see it, she crossed her middle finger over her index finger. She brushed her hand
against Alan's thigh, causing him to glance down.

It took an instant but he remembered their old signal, let's get out of here. They used it when they were
kids as sort of a question, when they were at someone's home or cottage and bored and wanted to know
if the other one was ready to leave. Then she pointed
to the car window and made a curious waving or swirling motion. It was obvious by Alan's expression he
had no idea what she was trying to say. Get out of
here—he recognized the signal, sure, but how? The
car window?

Not yet, she thought, but it's going to have to be very soon. Lorenzo wouldn't lead them a longer distance than he had to. He was looking for his spot and she was searching for hers. There? No. Up ahead there? Maybe. She swallowed. She couldn't risk waiting any longer. She slowed the car even more.

A moment later Sam was protesting, ''Hey, he's getting too far in front. Catch up.''

Mickey nodded her head. Obediently she started to accelerate rapidly. Every muscle in her body went rigid. Her hands tried to squeeze the steering wheel into dust. The car rocked and jolted along the rough road. They caught up to the sandstorm behind Lorenzo.

Sam's eyes tightened. ''Now what the devil are you trying to do? What . . .''

''He's too far ahead,'' Mickey screamed. ''I don't want to lose him. You said . . .'' Just a bit farther, she cautioned herself over and over again. Not yet, just a bit farther.

''That's too, hey, slow—'' Sam yelled back at her. His voice was almost drowned out by the roar of the car thrashing along the rough road. Clouds of fine dust streamed in the open windows.

Sam leaned forward, his pistol dancing in the air near her right ear. ''Stop this,'' he yelled. ''Stop!''

''Okay,'' Mickey screamed. ''Okay.'' But she gunned the motor. She gave the steering wheel a sharp jerk. The motor roared. Mickey's foot squeezed the gas pedal down to the floor.

The car lurched sideways, skidded off the edge of the road, whumped into a shallow ditch—the bottom of the car smacked down hard—then they surged up the smooth rock bank on the other side, and at the top tore through a thin veil of sumac bushes. Branches slapped at the car, cracking, then the furor stopped and they flew, motor wailing, wheels spinning uselessly, over a smooth cliff twenty feet in the air.

Waiting, body taut—it took so long—her knuckles shaded white as they braced on the steering wheel. A final breath was caught prisoner in her throat. She had chosen this course of action. She had aimed the car for the cliff, pumped the accelerator. Now she was helpless. There was nothing more she could do.

The car rolled. Limbs flailed about like those of rag dolls. Then the car suddenly stopped with an explosive crunch. Necks and shoulders and legs shot forward, then cracked back against seats and doors.

At first she couldn't focus and see. The car bobbed like a boat. Something was wrong. The motor still raced. The wheels still spun in the air. Mickey dangled, suspended by her seat belt. When she finally managed to breathe and open her eyes she was looking at black water through the windshield. She was dazed, disoriented.

They were upside down. The car had landed on its back and begun to roll forward. The bobbing eased.

The motor stopped with a sizzle. Everything went still. Mickey felt relief. She breathed deeply. Were they all right? She glanced at Alan. Woozy, he hung beside her. His head slowly oscillating from side to side. Where was Sam? She knew he hadn't bothered with a seat belt. She turned to look but stopped. A generous belch erupted from under the hood. Mickey emitted a startled cry. The car shimmied, and dove frontfirst deep into the water, plunging for the bottom. Water rushed in the open windows. Slowly spinning, the car drove down into the blackness, suddenly plunging like a stone. Scrambling, Mickey tried to find a way out. Water surged around her. She stole a last gasp of air. She was under. The water was icy cold. She couldn't force open the door. She couldn't see in the blackness. Clawing at the open window, she pulled, yanked, tried to kick her feet, tried to break free. Her ears popped from the rapidly increasing water pressure. She felt hands fumbling around her waist. She pushed the hands away. She had to breathe.

Don't panic, can't panic, the thoughts ricocheted through her mind, *have to get out, can't panic.* But it was useless, she had to breathe. Like a tidal wave, panic was threatening to overwhelm her.

She couldn't wait any longer. Frantically she lashed out in all directions. The hands were around her waist again. With one hand she tried to push them away. With the other hand she grabbed at the rim around the car window and pulled. She couldn't move. *What have*

I done? she screamed at herself. What have I done? She clenched her eyes and just shook madly. She had to breathe.

Then the straps of the seat belt went loose. She could move, but she was still stuck inside the car. The ceiling pushed down upon her head. She kicked and flailed, hit the steering wheel, the seats. She couldn't find the window. She had to breathe.

Someone caught her hand. She knew by the gentle touch it was Alan, trying to lead her. She recoiled from him. He grabbed her again. He wouldn't let go. He was pulling her the wrong way. She struggled, wiggling like a fish caught on a hook. Somehow she had to breathe.

He kept pulling and she kept trying to wriggle away. Her arms and legs and head kept bashing against the insides of the car. She hit something every time she moved. She couldn't hold her breath any longer, she had to open her mouth. She wanted to scream. She wanted to breathe. She wanted to cry. She had to breathe—she had to breathe now.

He still held her hand tight. He pulled.

It was all black, black. She couldn't see anything. Nothing at all, just blackness. Her head was caught by the edge of the window. He yanked harder. Her arm was stretching. She bent away. Suddenly, she was free. Her arms and legs could extend. They hit nothing. She looked around wildly. It was pitch-black, she couldn't even see her own arms. Where's the surface? Which way is up?

I have to breathe, I can't breathe, wait, wait—I need air. Fighting all her instincts she clenched her teeth and kept her mouth shut. Alan still held her hand. Now she held his so tight he couldn't have let go had he wanted to. He pulled her into the darkness. She swam as fast as she could, legs kicking wildly, her body writhing. Her chest and throat screamed to breathe; they threatened to explode.

Above there was a glimmer of silver—the surface, she could see it. She let go of his hand and they both swam madly. Light—she could see again. She could see her hands, her arms. She could see Alan. *Only a bit farther, hold on,* she begged, *swim.*

Finally they burst through the surface, gagging uncontrollably for air. Chests heaving, hurting, sucking in and out as fast as they could. They couldn't breathe fast enough. Each rush of air said, you're going to be okay, yes, going to be okay, yes . . .

"What were you doing?" Alan choked out.

She gasped for breath.

"What were you doing?" he shouted.

He was upset, she realized. Why was he upset? They got away, didn't they? Still, she couldn't say anything. She was too busy gobbling up air.

Alan jerked his head around and looked behind her. Then he grabbed her shoulders and pushed her back under.

Water caught in her throat. She gagged. She struggled from his grasp back to the surface. She snatched another quick breath of air. But he dragged her down again.

What was *he* doing, she demanded in a silent frenzy. Was Alan trying to kill her? Didn't he understand? He was still dragging her down, trying to swim underwater. Didn't he know she needed more oxygen? She struggled free and clawed to the surface again. She gasped, sucking in as much air as she could to her screaming lungs. Alan burst to the surface beside her, gasping for relief and yelling at her at the same time.

"Shooting . . . at . . ."

He tugged at her again. Mickey twisted away, and for a fleeting moment she saw Lorenzo standing on the shore atop a smooth rock ledge. He was aiming his gun at her. There was a sharp crack. Instantly, a splash erupted inches before her eyes. She struggled to follow Alan as quickly underwater as she could. She saw another violent spurt in front of her, a streak of bubbles, a tiny sinister bullet suddenly appeared, abruptly slowed and sank away benignly.

Together, side by side now, they swam beneath the surface for thirty feet. The last ounce of oxygen was wrung from her tortured chest. Only then did they dare emerge, sucking in one huge gasp of life-sustaining air before quickly diving. They did it again, and again. Establishing a rhythm, each time becoming a little easier—until Alan reached out for her hand and grabbed it as she started to dive under. He held it tightly.

Panting, she looked back at him. Her body shook. He too was panting, but still swimming slowly on the surface. She joined him. Neither of them spoke, each concerned only with gorging on sweet, delicious air.

Starting to feel better, Mickey looked back across the placid black water. There, on a ledge of pink-and-silver granite, one small figure was still discernible, standing high above the shore.

What next? she wondered.

Finally they reached the other side of the lake. She stood on a large slippery rock waist-deep in the water. Her legs felt like jelly; she flopped forward and rolled over onto her back. Safe, at last, she looked back across the lake. Safe, at least for the moment. Alan walked in the shallow water beside her. Swimming a few yards farther, Mickey pulled herself out of the lake and onto a large, smooth, dry slab of granite and lay panting with her face down, head resting in the nest formed by her folded arms.

Alan came to her; he put a hand on her shoulder, and drew it away again when she opened her eyes.

"I guess you had a perfectly good reason for racing over a cliff into a lake and almost killing us," he said. "Why did you do that?"

"I'm sorry it was the only way I could think of to get away."

Alan remained calm. "Killed. Drowned. Do you understand? They can't drag you back to Brazil. Not if you don't want to go. You're in Canada now. We have laws.''

"Alan, they weren't talking about how to get me back to Brazil and back to Max. They were talking about how best to murder us and hide the bodies so they could get away.''

"That's crazy,'' he muttered. "They weren't trying to kill us until you pulled that crazy stunt. They were just trying to scare you. So you'd do what they wanted.'' He turned away.

"No, I heard them. They were going to murder us,'' Mickey insisted.

He swung back toward her. "Oh, come on, be serious. All because he thinks he loves you, all because you left him?'' Already he was suspecting that he might be wrong, but he fought against the feeling. Murder: It was just so difficult to concede that someone was determined to kill him and Mickey.

"I don't understand it either, but they sure weren't driving us to any airport, were they?''

Alan did not answer. He considered what she said. His anger became frustration. "Why didn't they just kill us where we were? Why wait for the sun to rise? Why wait?''

"Lorenzo wanted to be farther away from the highway. I heard that much. He's careful. He wanted a deep lake, to hide the car and the bodies. Listen, Lorenzo knows what he is doing. They saw us in Sandhurst, they followed us all day, waiting for just the right moment. I saw that car in Sandhurst.''

Exhausted, Alan sank down on the rock beside her. He collapsed and closed his eyes and slowly shook his head.

''Alan, please, I know what I heard. They were discussing how to kill us, both of us, and where to dispose of the bodies—deep in the bush two bodies and a car dumped in the bottom of a deep lake would most likely never be found.''

The anger vanished. Now Alan's voice was tired and despondent. ''Are you absolutely sure?''

''Yes.''

''Do you speak Portuguese?'' he asked.

''Yes, well, a little, enough. It's a bit like Spanish. I can't really speak it, but . . .''

''But . . .''

''Alan, maybe I didn't catch all of it, but I'm sure of what I heard. They were deciding the best way to kill us and get rid of our bodies, and your car, and how they were going to get back to Brazil. That's all.''

''Why? But that's not what . . . This . . .'' He shook his head in frustration. ''Why do they want to kill you?''

''I don't know,'' Mickey said. ''Look, I'm sorry. I'm sorry I got you into this whole mess. I almost killed us driving the car off the cliff. I had to do something. I wasn't going to just sit around waiting to be slaughtered. I couldn't think of anything better and . . .''

''And it worked,'' he concurred.

There was a pause before she added, ''Come on.'' Mickey crawled up onto a higher rock beside a windbent and stunted jack pine tree. She felt more comfortable there completely out of sight of the man on the other side of the lake. She was exhausted. Her body ached everywhere. She felt as if she had gone through all the cycles inside a washing machine and then swam a marathon. She felt as if she would never catch her breath again.

Alan followed her. ''Look,'' he said, ''I'm the one that should apologize. I should have trusted that you knew what you were doing. It's just . . . I'm not used to this sort of stuff.''

''I'm not either, you know.''

Mickey turned toward him. ''Now what do we do?''

''Well, what was the second part of your plan?'' Alan asked, an overtly thoughtful expression almost hiding a hint of tired whimsy.

''There, um, was no second part.''

A slight smile creased his pensive countenance. His eyes met hers, and they grinned in unison.

Mickey continued, ''I figure it's your turn now. I got us this far.''

''And a marvelous job indeed.'' He was smiling broadly now. ''Just out of sight of a maniac with a gun intent on killing us for no discernible reason, we're stranded in the deep bush with nothing to our names save T-shirts, shorts, and running shoes, all very soggy.''

''Sorry.''

''I'm not.'' He chuckled softly and rocked toward her; for a moment Mickey thought he intended to kiss her. She moved back a bit in surprise. Instead he only propped himself up on one elbow and surveyed their surroundings. He avoided looking at her and seemed lost in thought.

''I guess we've got to get away from here, put some breathing space between your buddy and ourselves. I don't know how. Then maybe we can take another crack at finding out what is going on.''

Mickey looked into the bush. ''Maybe we should wait, then swim back across when he's gone. That way we wouldn't get lost out here in the middle of nowhere.''

Alan mulled the idea over. He drooped down and rolled over to lie flat on his back, gazing up at the sun, still taking full deep breaths. Then he swung over onto his side and looked out once more across the water. It was a large lake, long and narrow, winding out of sight both to his right and left, and possibly one-half mile across. A half mile of water separated them from Lorenzo. He tilted his head and peered through the tree branches until he could see the car. They were safe where they were. It didn't appear possible for Lorenzo to find a way to drive the car around the lake, not easily, anyway. Would he try swimming after them? No, not likely, but it was hard to be certain. The idea of them swimming back to the other side and hoping he wasn't there waiting for them wasn't at all appealing.

"No," Alan decided. "I don't want to risk going back and meeting your friend again. And I don't think we should wait here too long. I'd rather try my luck with the bears." And he nodded toward the bush.

"Bears?" Mickey asked.

Alan couldn't help but smile at the way she found the energy to snap her head up and quickly search the forest shadows. "Bears," he stated, "will be the least of our worries. Finding our way out of here will be the real challenge. It could be a long walk. There is nothing up here. Just bush and more bush. And I don't know if I want to go back to that highway."

Mickey said, "That's probably what Lorenzo will expect us to do."

"Yes. Maybe we'll get lucky and find a fishing camp or something."

"Or a resort with a salad bar."

"I'd be satisfied with a telephone."

"We could order pizza."

"Let me guess, you're feeling a little peckish."

"Starving."

There was no easy answer for that. They both thought ravenously of that poor jar of peanut butter

and loaf of bread in the back of Alan's car, now resting in the depths of a very deep lake.

Basking in the warm sun for ten minutes slowly
baked the deep chill out of their severely abused bodies. Then, without a word passing between them, they
got to their feet together and started to walk. Sore and
exhausted, still damp, their legs as wobbly as thin
stalks of rubber, they had no choice but to drag themselves off into the bush.

They decided to head west if they could, parallel to
the highway. They used the sun to keep their bearings.

They didn't talk, it was too tiring. In their condition
walking would be challenge enough, and this was an
obstacle course: dodging trees; leaping over cracks and
fissures; ducking and breaking through pine branches,
sumacs, and poplar saplings; skidding on steep, lichen-
covered granite; lunging down to crevices filled with
dead pine needles; veering around swamps and im-
pregnable thorny bushes; scrambling up ridges—
sometimes they were rewarded by a few short steps
on the crest of a high, skull-like rock with a sweeping
vista of vivid green, blue, pink, and purple in a wild
and erratic design.

When they came to yet another river, Alan said, as
he waded in without hesitation, ''What I wouldn't give
for a canoe.''

Mickey cupped the water in her hands and drank.
''Or a peanut butter sandwich.''

They swam to the other side and kept on going,

breaking back into the forest. They met no bears, but twice they saw deer, once in the distance across a small lake. The dark-eyed creatures just watched their progress, content that they were safe. The other time Mickey and Alan startled a family that fled out of a thicket of white birch right in front of them. Like a camera flash the animals were there, then gone. It was hard to tell who had been the more frightened, the deer or the people.

Neither Alan nor Mickey suggested stopping for a break. Both were afraid if they did stop they wouldn't have the energy to start walking again.

Despite their best efforts, by midafternoon, while they may have wandered for ten miles, they hadn't managed five as the crow flies. The plan wouldn't work; they'd die out here. Heading back to the highway and praying Lorenzo wasn't out there cruising for them, risky as it seemed, began to look like the better option—if they could find the highway, that is. Both had the same thoughts. Alan was leading; the path he chose was always west but tended to angle a little to the south, toward the highway. Mickey noticed and silently agreed.

Then their spirits soared. They broke through a wall of bramble bushes, thorns nipping at their skin and clothes, and there on the other side was a wide, flat, open section. It had obviously been recently lumbered out. Not only was the traveling easy over the flat, fairly clear field, but there was the possibility of a road and, perhaps most important of all, there were endless blueberries. Not enough to sustain life, but a welcome lift to their sagging spirits. It was still very early in the season, and most of the berries were hard green little gems, but some were dark blue, swollen up rich and plump and juicy.

They ate as they walked, eyes down, searching each plant for the bulging dark berries that were ready and sweet. Sporadically stooping and snatching up the tiny meal, popping it in their mouths for a short burst of delicious musky flavor. They looked like two farmyard chickens out for a stroll, pecking at the ground.

Simultaneously they stopped. In the distance they heard a faint rumbling. It rapidly grew more and more intense. They looked at each other. The earth shook. Then it burst upon them, charging across the edge of their field. From behind a screen of poplars, not fifty yards away, a huge train barreled into view, rushing by, car after car. Instinctively they ran toward it, frantically waving and screaming. The train was gone well before they reached the tracks. The only sign it had ever been there was the ringing in their ears and the trembling in their weary limbs.

When Mickey reached the shiny steel ribbon, she plopped down on the track and announced, ''I'm not going another step. The next train that comes by I'm going to hop on.''

''You have got to be kidding. Did you see how fast

that train was going? There is no way you are going to jump aboard.''

"I'll get them to stop."

"Yeah, right. Even if someone happens to see you waving, they'll just think you're being friendly.''

Mickey frowned. She knew he was right. "Well, I can't move anymore. I'm going to lie here then, across these tracks, and hope some gallant hero saves me.''

Alan was peering in both directions down the rail bed. He looked back at her. "Well, it won't be me, because I'm going to follow these tracks.''

"No," she protested. "Tell me we don't have to?''

He shrugged. "They must lead somewhere.''

"Sure they do. Winnipeg, just a thousand miles.''

"Oh, come on, it can't be more than four or five hundred. We can jog there in . . . three, four weeks.'' He tried to laugh, but it took too much energy.

Mickey's head sank into her hands. Her elbows were propped up on her knees, and her arms formed a crutch for the weight of her head. She closed her eyes, resting.

Alan sat beside her on the rail. He moved off and tried to get more comfortable sitting on the black, creosote-soaked railway tie and leaning up against the rail. Still not satisfied, he stretched out flat on the gravel rail bed.

Mickey's eyes didn't open. "What I wouldn't give for a Tempest right now," she said in a dreamy voice.

Alan responded, "What I wouldn't give to be able to give you one."

"If you gave me one I'd share it with you."

"Thanks." He smiled. "I appreciate that."

Mmm, a Tempest, just dreaming about it was sort of satisfying, rich and thick and cool, and creamy, and . . .

Mickey started. She spun around to stare into the bush behind her. "Did you hear something?" she whispered.

Alan hauled himself up onto one elbow and looked down the tracks.

"No," Mickey advised in a hushed voice. "Not another train—something over there in the bushes."

There was an unmistakable rustling in a large shrubby clump, twenty feet away.

"Do you think it could be a bear?" Mickey asked.

"No. Well, I guess it could be. Bear, wolf, moose . . ." Lorenzo?

They crouched down, tense, ready to spring to their feet and flee. The rustling came closer. They still couldn't see anything.

Five feet in front of them the tips of the tall weeds quivered. Mickey pulled her legs up under her. Then, right before them, they were face-to-face with a pair of small black eyes and a wide smile—a furry animal, jet black save for a thick white double stripe that began on the crown of his head and ran all the way down its back.

Alan laughed. "Why it's just a—"

Mickey sprang to her feet and bolted down the tracks. "Skunk!" she emitted in voice that was both screaming in panic and hushed at the same time.

"Oh, no," Alan muttered and he scrambled after her. He took three quick steps on the loose gravel and stumbled.

Mickey came back to him, offering her hand. "Come on, hurry up, hurry," she insisted.

Quite unperturbed, the skunk meandered out onto the tracks and watched the escape. Then he turned his backside to them and wandered calmly across the tracks and back into the tall grass.

Gradually their mad dash slowed to a run, a trot, a listless jog, then they walked, trying to maintain a brisk pace but inevitably going slower and slower.

Mickey finally started to laugh. "You should have seen your face when you finally realized it was a skunk."

Alan answered between gasps. "I thought, it was, just a, cute little . . . animal."

"It was cute. Cute and more dangerous than a bear. At least if we were eaten by a bear it would have solved most of our problems. We wouldn't have had to worry about Lorenzo, or food. . . . I think being sprayed by a skunk on top of all this would have been just too much for me to take. Can you imagine?" She couldn't help laughing. "And I don't know why I'm laughing, it's not in the least bit funny.'' The run and the resulting fatigue had left her feeling a little giddy.

They kept walking along the railway line. It was easier going than the constant dodging of trees, rocks, and crevices in the bush.

''You know, should we be following the tracks? It might make it easier for Lorenzo to find us,'' Mickey considered.

''It's better than dying out here in the bush. I don't think there is anything around other than the railway. We were very lucky just to stumble upon it.''

The sun beat down upon their tired backs. Overhead a hawk glided, effortlessly circling high in the air.

Mickey saw it first. ''I wish we could do that,'' she said. ''Beautiful . . . Do you think he's got his eyes on us? You know, waiting for us to collapse?''

Alan looked up but kept walking.

''I'm sorry about your car,'' Mickey announced.

Alan exhaled a little smile. ''It's okay. I just wonder if my insurance will cover intentionally driving into a bottomless lake.''

Mickey looked again back over her shoulder.

''There is no way they can find us here,'' Alan assured her.

''It's not just Lorenzo I'm worried about,'' Mickey responded.

''What then?''

Mickey shrugged her shoulders. ''Another train might come.''

"I guess that's possible." He smiled.

"And I still want to figure out a way to get on."

He shook his head. "At the next station."

"Winnipeg."

"No, when you think about it there could be a little settlement around the next bend. There are a few I think, sort of left over from the old days along the rail line." The thought was encouraging.

The sun had slipped well past its zenith. The shadows were beginning to get longer. It was still hot and humid. Not a hint of a breeze stirred the air to cool them.

Mickey tried to rest her eyes by closing them and walking on blindly for a few steps. It was a brief respite until she would stumble and have to open them again.

"Alan, do you think Sam drowned?" She asked suddenly.

At first Alan didn't answer. It was as though he didn't hear her question. "I don't know," he said eventually. "I was wondering about that when we were walking in the bush. I think he must have. We didn't see any sign of him."

"We almost drowned."

"Yes."

"He is a pretty good swimmer, though. Sometimes he or Lorenzo would pace Max in his morning workouts. Usually it was me. In fact that's how I got away.

. . . You know, it was really only the day before yesterday. Incredible.''

Mickey shook her head. She faltered for a second and almost stopped walking. She raised her arms up in front of her. She was so tired her bones, especially her elbows and shoulders, felt as if they were vibrating, humming like a tuning fork. Taking a deep breath, she started to speak again as though she had decided talking would keep her mind off of how sore and exhausted she was. She rambled on. ''During the day Max never let me out of his sight. Even when he did his morning laps in the pool I had to swim with him. Either I or one of the bodyguards—Lorenzo or Sam— would pace him. That's who Lorenzo and Sam are— Max's bodyguards and sort-of assistants. They do whatever he tells them. He used to love to beat them at things, games, sports. Max was a good swimmer. Actually, I think the bodyguards were smart enough to put up a good show, and then always let Max win. But I don't know.''

She looked back over her shoulder. ''The day I left I complained of cramps and got out. Sam and Lorenzo got into the pool to keep him company. It was just the chance I was waiting for. It was odd for all three of them to be in the pool, and even stranger that nobody was in the house. I couldn't believe my luck. It couldn't have been better if I had arranged it all. I sat at the end with my legs in the water so Max could know where I was, so he wouldn't tell one of them to keep an eye on me. When they completed one lap and started to swim away, I took off. I never looked back. I was all ready. My knapsack was packed and stashed in a closet. I took a taxi directly to the airport. I was still wearing my wet bathing suit under my T-shirt and shorts when I got there. I changed in the washroom while I was waiting for my flight. I had intended to go back to L.A. or maybe to my sister's in Vancouver, then I saw the Toronto flight, and just had an urge. I thought I was completely free of them when I got on the plane. I was so happy, coming home and all.''

"Then for some reason they came after you."

"Then for some reason they came after me, yes."

Alan wiped the sweat from his forehead with his right hand. "While we're walking let's see if we can't figure this thing out. I mean, they weren't trying to take you back to Max, were they? Why were they trying to kill—"

"I've gone over it a thousand times."

"Well, maybe a different perspective . . . Why come after you? Why do they want to kill us?"

"I don't know."

"Why does anyone kill someone? They only wanted to kill me because I was with you. They could hardly kill you now and leave me alone."

"I'm sorry."

"Look, quit saying that, it's not your fault," he said. "You have nothing to be sorry for."

"Look what I've done to your life."

"You've certainly made it a whole lot more exciting."

"And a whole lot shorter too, maybe."

"No, we can beat this. Let's see if we can figure out why they want you dead."

"Oh, Alan, I just don't know. I can't think of anything."

"Let's do this logically. They must have a reason, right? They aren't just doing this for fun."

"No, they must have a reason. These guys aren't crazy—well, they are a little crazy, but they aren't sick, kill-for-fun types. They are very cold and calculating, especially Max.... And Lorenzo is scary and ruthless, but not sick like that."

"Okay, why then does anyone want to kill someone, not just you, anyone?"

"I don't know, I've never had the urge to kill anyone. Revenge, I suppose. Greed, hate ..." She shrugged. She didn't know why people would intentionally murder someone. But they do, Mickey reminded herself. "Self-defense?"

"Hardly, in this case."

"I know."

They were still walking steadily. "Maybe to eliminate a threat," Alan said thoughtfully.

Mickey looked over at Alan. "He may hate me," she said, "but not enough to kill me, and I am hardly a threat to him. I don't know. I'm too tired."

"Do you think maybe, I don't know, maybe there

is something you know, that you don't know you
know, you know what I mean? Something that might
be a threat to Max, something you know about him.''

''Can you say that again?''

''Something about Max you know, something important, but something you may not even know you
know.''

''That's what I thought you said.'' Mickey started
to laugh and stopped abruptly. ''Oh, it hurts when I
laugh, please don't make me laugh.''

''Something Max doesn't want anyone else to
know, like . . . well, I don't know, some business se-
crets maybe.''

''I suppose there could be something. But Max
never told me anything about his business or anything
like that. He was very secretive. He said he was an
entrepreneur. That's all. I suspect it was probably a
pretty shady operation, but I can't think of anything
that I know that might be a secret or damaging to him.
He didn't tell me anything. I don't know if he was a
drug dealer, or a store owner, or a stockbroker, or all
of them. I'm sure I don't know any secret codes, or
names, or places. He didn't tell me anything.''

It was too exhausting to concentrate. No fresh ideas
sprang into her mind.

''Maybe he wants something . . . maybe he has a
life insurance policy on you,'' Alan said with a re-
signed voice. ''Simple enough. You die, he collects.''

Mickey smiled. "I don't think so. He hardly needs the money."

Alan found the energy to clench his fist. "Think. There must be some reason."

Baffled, they walked on in silence for half a mile.

"Are you angry at me?" Mickey asked.

"No, I just can't help wondering if there isn't something you aren't telling me."

"Alan. I wouldn't lie or anything."

"I know. I mean something you don't realize you know."

"Here we go again."

He stumbled, riding over on his ankle, twisting it. He hopped for two steps but carried on. "This is so weird. My life is usually pretty logical, pretty dull in comparison."

"Sounds heavenly."

"Well, since you've come back people have tried to kill us. . . . That's never happened before."

"But, Alan . . ."

"And I don't know why. It'd be nice to know why." He looked over at her. His face was tired, verging on defeated; then he grinned, exhaled, and shook his head.

Mickey tried to smile. Then she continued in a compassionate voice, "Alan, I am so sorry I got you into this mess."

"You've already said that. And it's not your fault." Alan took a deep, weary breath. "Besides, I should point out that there are certain aspects of my present predicament that I am quite happy about. In fact, in some respects I have never been happier.'' He reached out and took her hand. ''And another thing, I wish they would space these stupid railway ties to make it easier to walk on them. They are either too close together, or just too far apart for a proper stride.''

Mickey squeezed his hand and kept it in her grasp. She stepped up onto the rail and tried walking along its smooth, narrow path. After five steps she tottered and had to step down.

''Maybe we should sing songs,'' Alan said with a chuckle.

''Oh, please, no,'' Mickey protested.

''You know, like . . .'' He started to sing in a thundering voice. ''I've been walking on the railroad, all the livelong day. . . .'' He gasped and took a deep breath. ''Everybody now, I've been walking on the railroad. . . .'' He bellowed like an opera singer. His arms spread out like wings. Then he stopped completely. His booming voice vanished into the quiet, desolate bush.

Mickey was feeling giddy; she started to giggle.

''That's all the words I can remember,'' Alan said in confusion. ''How does the rest of it go?''

''Don't make me laugh.''

''There you go, laughing like a seal again.''

"Oh, no, don't. I can't walk and laugh at the same time. It hurts, laughing is agony."

Alan took her hand in his and kissed it. He continued to hold it as they kept on walking.

"From now on, I concentrate on the positive, the good things. Like"—and his voice went overtly dreamy—"I am all alone with the beauteous Mickey Chapeskie and holding her hand." He smiled into space but didn't look at her.

"All alone is an understatement, I'd say, you lucky guy," Mickey said. Then she continued. "I think the heat is getting to us, you especially," Mickey said. "We are starting to babble like fools."

"Happy fools, laughing at danger, dancing with death."

"Well, I'd rather have a burger, a bath, and a bed. Make that two burgers."

"Where's a McDonald's when you need one?"

By late afternoon they came to a narrow bridge. It was more than a hundred yards long and spanned a steep-sided gorge. A small stream only dampened the rocky carpet at the bottom.

"We can't cross this," Mickey insisted. "Trains always come just as you reach halfway."

"What choice do we have?" Alan responded. "We can hardly stay here. We certainly don't want to climb down and cross the riverbed; that would take forever."

"I think we should wait. I think we have to rest a bit. I'm too tired to carry on."

With an effort Alan swallowed. His throat was parched. He looked down into the gorge at the trickle of water and wondered how hard it would be to climb down. A foolish idea, he concluded. "You're right," he complained with resignation. "We need a rest."

"Just a little while, okay?" Mickey suggested. She held his hand and led the way down from the tracks over to a large stone bluff jutting out into the gorge.

"Maybe it would be safe to cross right after a train. They wouldn't schedule two trains close together," Alan mumbled halfheartedly as though trying to convince himself it was wise to wait. He knew once they stopped it would be difficult to get moving again. He knew that they had, in effect, stopped for the night and he didn't have any ideas on how to build a little shelter or find food or make a fire, and didn't have the energy to do so. Maybe it would be wise to rest for a while, then walk on in the cool moonlight.

Collapsing on the ledge, they lay, Alan facedown, his head resting on his crossed arms, Mickey on her back, her hands folded neatly on her lap. Breathing deeply, they did not stir until Mickey rolled and twisted her head around to look at the bridge.

"Alan, that bridge is pretty old, isn't it?"

Alan just groaned in response. He was trying to remember those boy scout tricks for making a fire and a lean-to. There could be animals at night, and doubtless they'd both sleep like rocks. He had almost decided he'd see what kind of refuge he could make out of pine branches when she spoke.

"Do you think," Mickey continued, "a train, maybe a big freight train, would have to slow down to cross over it, you know, for safety reasons?"

Lifting his head, Alan looked at the bridge. He tried to inspect it like an expert. It was old, and amazingly narrow, no guardrails or shoulder like a highway—not that a train needed that sort of thing, still it looked so incredibly precarious. "I don't know. Maybe." His head sank back onto his arms. His eyes closed.

Slowly getting up, Mickey went back to the railroad tracks. She put her hand on the shiny rail. She couldn't detect any vibration. Looking up and down the rails she chose a spot nearby where the tracks passed over a large, even surface covered with rock and thin moss. She walked over to it. The flat run was at least thirty feet in length, and slanted down gradually, ending flush with the rail bed. Sitting there cross-legged, rocking back and forth, she considered what she saw.

Alan came and sat beside her.

"When the next train comes I'm going to try to run and catch it," she announced.

Alan shook his head. He looked around, trying hard to think. He didn't know what to say. "Yes, well, I guess it's worth a try," he concurred, "maybe it will slow down enough." But he didn't sound convinced.

Side by side they sat and waited and dozed. The sun began its final descent. No trains came. Every twenty minutes or so Mickey got to her feet and stretched just like a sprinter getting ready for the hundred-yard dash, except unlike a sprinter, with every effort she grimaced in pain.

The next train came just after the sun had set behind the west lip of the gorge. The sky still glimmered with fading lavender. The forest was ensconced in dark and long murky shadows.

Mickey leaped to her feet. "Do you hear it?" She shouted, "Alan, do you hear it?" She ran up and touched the rail. "It's shaking. A train is coming. It is." She hastened back to where he was sleeping and cajoled him to his feet by tugging on his shoulder. "Come on, get ready."

He staggered to his feet and followed her back to the end of the long smooth rock she had selected as their launching ramp. The rumble grew louder. They waited. A blinding light swept across a bend farther down the track.

Mickey started hopping up and down on her toes, trying to loosen up her muscles. "Get ready," she insisted. "Are you ready?"

Alan nodded. He bent over at the waist several times. He quavered. Three hops on his toes he managed before he stopped and winced. He tried to shake the dust out of his head.

"It's going slower, isn't it?" she yelled.

"Sure," Alan answered in a noncommittal voice.

But it did seem to be going slow, maybe even slow enough.

The engine, then another, three engines thundered past, shaking the earth and creating a frightful din.

"Come on," Mickey called out. Then she sprinted forward along the rock as fast as she could. Alan followed three feet behind.

She raced, going almost as fast as the train, then she was alongside. It was a freight train. Boxcars streamed by. She chose a car, a railing to grab hold of, a stair to jump onto. Reaching out in the gray failing light, only a foot away, stretching to gain the last few inches, close . . . She stumbled, plunging to the loose gravel rail bed, landing hard in the gravel, mere inches from the great clashing steel wheels of the boxcars. Her arms lashed out to break her fall. She suddenly felt a rush of air and jerked her left arm back from the blur of the great huge wheels. Her knees bled.

Alan was at her side, trying to pull her back and help her up.

Mickey lay frozen in terror, staring, mesmerized by the gnashing of the huge steel wheels. She was afraid to move. She couldn't. The huge train generated a fierce wind that swirled around her, tearing at her hair, flapping the edge of her clothes. She wasn't going to move again until the train was long gone.

"Get up," he yelled. He sprang to his feet beside her. "You almost had it. We can do it." The noise of steel crushing steel was deafening. He had to scream to be heard.

Mickey let herself be pulled to her feet. She followed obediently back ten, twenty, thirty feet on the rock. She didn't want to try again. She was scared. It was dark. The train was so menacingly huge and uncaring. It kept rushing by. She hadn't realized before how impossible it would be. One slip, one little mistake and you could be dead, crushed, unnoticed, chopped up beneath those relentless wheels.

Alan ran first. Jogging loosely behind, Mickey watched him. She didn't want to try again, but she didn't want him to get away. A string of empty flatbeds were passing now. He was alongside the tail end of one. He reached out, the gravel shifted beneath his feet. He did not stumble, but he missed his chance. He slowed. The front end of the next car came by. He jumped and grabbed hold of the iron balustrade. He swung in the air, his feet fumbling for the rung of a step.

Mickey watched in horrified amazement. He can't leave me here. She ran faster. He can't leave me here alone.

He had his footing now, holding tightly with one hand he reached back with his other.

''Come on, you can do it,'' he implored her.

She didn't hear him. His words were washed away by the wind and drowned by the noise. She concentrated on reaching the train, reaching his hand, not falling—staying away from those wheels. She was close. Very close. An argument raged inside her; she'd be safe if she just stopped, she'd be alone if she didn't jump. At the last possible moment she leaped and caught his grasp. Their hands clenched in a desperate, tenacious grip.

Already they were crossing the long narrow bridge. She was dangling from his arm. Falling now would be certain death—a long fall to the rocks below.

''Don't look down,'' he yelled.

Impulsively Mickey immediately glanced down at the bottom of the dark gorge below her.

Her feet flailed blindly in the breeze, searching tentatively, terrified of coming too close to the huge wheels, searching recklessly, anything to take the load off of her arm, anything to stop the wild flailing in empty space. She kicked at the steel lip of the flatbed. There was no ledge there—no step, no iron rung, only smooth steel and empty air—but there had to be. She couldn't hold on much longer. But she had to. She rested an instant, gritted her teeth, and summoned up what remaining energy she had for one last desperate try. Swinging her legs forward with all her might, her right foot caught something, the step; it slipped off, her left foot lashed out and caught hold, long enough to yank her right foot back and gain a good hold with her toes. She had it. Now both feet were on the step. Hc guided her hand to the iron balustrade. Both hands clenched the railing.

Beneath her feet the train sped over the last of the narrow bridge. Deep below the bridge she could just make out the rocky canyon floor. She almost swooned at the sight. But, determined, she looked away and very carefully followed Alan up over the side of the car. He rolled down onto the flatbed and waited with his arms out to catch her. She lunged.

They collapsed, flat, hugging the rough wood floor, huddled down behind the short forward wall of the flatbed. It served to break the wind a little, but still a swirling breeze surged over their bodies. Her hair whipped about. The loose hem of her yellow T-shirt continued to flutter in the breeze.

"Nothing to it," Alan said without a hint of mirth anywhere in his exhausted body.

"Piece of cake," Mickey responded. She trembled all over and repressed a tired whimper.

Exhausted, they lay side by side, but slowly the coolness of the evening air drew them closer together. Finally Mickey found herself snuggling half on top of him, seeking to tap the warmth of his body, the softness of his shoulder, the comfort of his silent strength. Despite the hunger, the trembling tiredness in her limbs, the still-pulsating fear, the confusion, the cold dankness of her clothes, the noise, and the ceaseless buffeting by the wind over the flatbed, nothing could be more wonderful than the soothing warmth of his body. She was amazingly comfortable, and calm, calmer than she could ever remember feeling. Was it just the fact that they were safe and speeding to civilization, food, and shelter? No, she realized suddenly, the force field was gone; maybe it was sheer fatigue, but there was no clumsy awkwardness between their bodies. They intermeshed tightly and cosily, like one. It was a delicious sensation, and whether it was just a temporary reprieve brought about by relief and exhaustion, or a fundamental change in their relationship, she didn't consider. For now she just luxuriated in it.

Mickey reached up, craning her neck, and kissed him below the ridge of his jaw. She wanted to kiss him on the lips, but she just couldn't manage to summon up that kind of energy. Besides, she thought to herself, he'll understand. Alan always seems to understand.

Chapter Four

Throughout the night, the fleet rhythm of the train provided a gentle, vibrating massage. Her tired body sank into a deep, delicious sleep, just short of total oblivion. Before the crack of sunrise the ride began to change, the swift smoothness was gradually replaced by a slow, clumsy jarring that shook her. She saw those faces again, Sam and Lorenzo, at the airport, on the plane, by the car, Lorenzo standing high upon the granite precipice. In her dream she zoomed in close to envisage furious anger tearing into his face. And as she struggled to awaken, her dream went like this. . . .

Max with a gleam in his eye grabbed her knee, squeezing roughly. Lorenzo and Sam, swimming in the pool on either side of him, smacked the concrete.

Shoulder to shoulder all three turned, whooshing away.

She saw herself, fleeing through the garden, heading for the house, running, refusing to look back, listening keenly for sounds of danger. She heard the steady rhythm of the swimmer's splashes. Suddenly the splashes became loud, frantic, insistent. They know, they know, they are coming after me—now what? She watched herself freeze, unable to move, unable to move, unable to move.

Mickey awoke with a kick and a shudder. She was disoriented and short of breath.

There was a series of distinct clacks and jolts as the train crossed a rusty steel bridge. She was safe, she remembered, on a moving freight train, outside in the open on a flatbed car, it was still dark, and she was with Alan—it still seemed like a strange dream.

She breathed deep and slow and full. Nuzzling into the cozy hollow of Alan's shoulder, she pulled shut her eyelids again.

A dew made their skin moist, their clothes clammy. A fine dust covered them from head to foot. The air was wonderfully fresh but cool.

"We're slowing down," Alan whispered.

She nodded. Her head barely moved.

The sky in the east was a tin gray varying to vacant black in the west. The dimness about the train was interrupted by street lamps with fuzzy halos and patches of light escaping from windows or glowing on signs and billboards. It was the fringe of a city. There was the irritating clang of a bell, brief red flashes, and the glimmer of headlights as a pickup truck waited at a level crossing while the train rumbled by. The scrubby bush and barren rock was gone. The land was fairly flat and open, a sea of lush green farmland. She could see the fences and fields, the old barns and rambling houses.

Her legs were stacked against one of his. Her right arm rested on his stomach. She could feel him breathe, his chest rising and falling slowly.

''Mickey?''

''Hmm.''

''Are you okay?'' he asked.

She nodded again. The unruly fluff of her hair brushed against fresh stubble on his chin and the ridge of his jaw. His gentle voice was a tonic. There wasn't another man she could possibly feel so safe with— more than safe, safe and happy, and thrilled.

''We should get off before someone discovers us,'' he said.

She nodded but didn't move. The ravages of their odyssey seemed to heighten his appeal. She lay there happy in the comfort of his arms and breathed him in.

''Don't you think we should?'' he asked.

She nodded again. And she allowed herself to wonder about her own bedraggled appearance. Alan's clothes were torn and filthy, his arms and legs were scratched and yet he looked . . . magnificent. She allowed her hand to drift along his chest and dally upon his smooth, taut stomach. She gave him a light pat.

Alan stirred. He kissed her on the top of her hair. "Come on," he whispered. "Up we get."

Mickey nodded. Parting from Alan was like breaking free from her life support system. Reluctantly she summoned up what energy she could muster and took a sharp breath; then, stiff and weak, she attempted to move. Her limbs threatened to snap like dead dry twigs as she strained to straighten them. Gingerly she rocked over onto her hands and knees and sank back down onto her haunches. The car swayed and it took a moment for her to gain her balance.

Oh, to be home, she pined. Sunrise, lounging on the front deck with Alan, a cup of steaming hot tea and a terribly fattening breakfast—home, she abruptly realized, in her dreams, had become Alan and Mariposa. The small apartment in West Hills, California, was a fading memory.

Alan staggered to his feet, rocked, took two steps to be steady, waited, then stretched his arms out, clenched his fists, and groaned mournfully, a long and hollow groan. Arms dangling at his sides, he looked down at his hands. "Tell me, is one of my arms about a foot longer than the other?" he asked, giving his left arm a shake, then rubbing first the elbow, then the shoulder. "I feel like a gorilla."

"How do you know what a gorilla feels like?" she

teased, but she spoke with such fatigue she managed only the smallest of smiles. Then the memory of being suspended by the grasp of his hand as the train crossed over the deep dark chasm engulfed her, and the vivid memories of the merciless gnashing of huge steel wheels close before her face, and the rush of the train's wind, the cold blackness of the water, the crash of the car, and the piercing pain in her chest from lack of air. ''You saved my life,'' she stated flatly.

He scoffed in response. ''Yeah, right. I almost killed you too. We must have been crazy. It was a reckless thing to do.'' Then he laughed weakly and added, ''It was a whole series of crazy reckless things to do.''

Mickey tried to smile. ''What choice did we have?''

And there was no arguing with that.

She rubbed the sleep out of her eyes with the heel of one hand.

Silver rails spread out row on row beside them. There were dirty red boxcars, black tankers, cattle cars, and long files of golden grain cars. Diesel fuel, old grease, and dust began to contaminate the air. The train had slowed to the speed of a brisk walk. Ribbons of tangerine and lavender entwined in the eastern sky, and the bright upper lip of the sun barely peeked over the wide horizon.

''Well,'' Alan said, ''I guess we'd better get out of here.'' Cautiously he moved closer to the edge of the car.

''I guess,'' Mickey agreed.

"There's probably a law against jumping freight trains." Alan gazed at the rough gravel road bed.

"I guess so," Mickey murmured with a tired shrug. She joined him near the edge.

Six feet beneath their toes, there was a deceptively slow passing collection of loose gravel, railway ties, tracks, and tufts of tall weeds—rough and shadowy.

"Together on three," Alan said. He held her hand. Mickey stared blankly at the ground, too drowsy to think. He swung their hands back and forth as he counted. "One, two, three . . ." She flinched, but they didn't jump. They looked at each other and both shook their heads.

"I figured if you jumped, I'd follow," Mickey said.

"I figured if you jumped, I'd follow," Alan repeated.

"I couldn't," Mickey said. "I'm not jumping. I'm too stiff. I'm tired of doing dangerous things."

"Maybe we shouldn't do anything hasty. I don't think we're really awake yet. This getting off—the train is hardly moving—it looks harder than hopping on." He took two steps back. He still held her hand.

"Under the circumstances I don't care if we get in any trouble for sneaking a ride," Mickey suggested. "I mean, after all we've been through. I think they'll understand."

"Yes. I guess you're right."

She scrunched up her shoulders and wiggled the

muscles in her legs. "I'm so stiff. I can feel every muscle in my body, and they are all complaining."

"Tell me about it."

"I'm in agony," she stated flatly without a hint of whining.

"On second thought, don't, maybe it will go away if we don't think about it."

"Yeah, right. Sure it will."

"Undoubtedly." He managed a feeble nod that was interrupted by a slow yawn that grew to an enormous stretch.

The train had almost come to a complete stop in the marshaling yards before they started to hobble down the iron rung ladder at the end of the car. Stumbling on the last step, Mickey started to fall, but Alan held her firmly. The train stopped with a jerk.

They had just reached the ground and moved away when the train, with a screech and a series of shudders, began to back up.

Walking stiffly, they crossed over pairs of shiny steel rails until a string of dull red boxcars blocked their path. Cutting between two, they climbed up on the steel coupling. It was caked thick with black grease and a hard crust of dirt. Alan and Mickey were acutely aware that at any moment the train might be shunted forward or back, with them sandwiched in between. Gobs of grease smeared their knees, hands, and the seats of their shorts as they hurried through.

After crossing a few more sets of tracks they came

to a wire fence at the edge of the rail yard. Mickey whisked her hair out of her face and left a greasy black smudge on her forehead. She wiped it and the blotch grew. She gave up.

Alan took a corner of his T-shirt and used it to try to clean the smear.

''I must look awful.''

''Yeah,'' he answered with a grin. ''Absolutely awful.'' His eyes sparkled. ''Absolutely gruesome—scary,'' he added. Then Alan dropped the corner of his shirt and with his fingertips coaxed the curve of her chin upward. Slowly he bent down to her. His lips brushed the rise of her cheek and kissed. Then he shuddered and grimaced and recoiled in mock terror. ''Absolutely hideous.'' His horror gradually transformed into a sparkling grin. ''I sure wish I had a camera.'' Mickey thumped him in the arm. ''Yes, a camera,'' she mocked, ''it's certainly the most important thing we could use right now.''

Alan turned away from Mickey to look at the fence. ''I guess we have to go up and over,'' he said before glancing back at her. But she had already started. At the top Mickey gingerly straddled the barbed wire, tottered a moment, and swung away; there was a rip, and she vaulted to the sidewalk. Tan cotton threads were left behind. It was just one more tear in her clothes. She was beyond caring.

After he had followed her over, Alan asked, ''Well,

what shall we do next? Police station or breakfast?''
Then he added, ''Or shower, or new clothes?''

Mickey didn't answer. She shrugged her shoulders.
She knew she needed to eat and get cleaned up—she
had never been this grungy in her life—but she didn't
want Alan to think she was avoiding going to the
police.

They had landed in loose gravel beside a paved road
that was much cratered, cracked, and patched. It separated the rail yard from a ramshackle neighborhood
of cement block buildings, some warehouses, a few
grimy industries. Many buildings were abandoned,
long empty with faded FOR SALE signs and tall, vig-
orously growing weeds. In the distance, in all directions, there was the rumble of trucks and the hum of
cars.

She asked, ''Any idea where we are?''

''Winnipeg?'' He shrugged.

''Not the nicest neighborhood.'' Mickey looked
around. ''But it looks terrific to me. No bears, no
skunks, no Lorenzo . . .''

''Hopefully, no Lorenzo.''

''Hopefully, no Lorenzo?'' The thought started her
thinking. Could Lorenzo possibly be here?

''I think we're safe now,'' Alan offered simply.

''Yes, but we've thought that before.''

''Nobody could follow us here.''

''Nobody would want to. They might be able to
anticipate where we would end up though.''

"I don't think so," Alan responded, but there was uncertainty in his voice.

"Never underestimate Lorenzo. He seems to have a knack of knowing what to do, and when to do it. Must be an instinct he was born with, or something he learned surviving in the São Paulo slums."

Both looked back over their shoulders. Could it be true? Could Lorenzo have predicted where they would end up? If he had had a map he'd have noticed the railway line running through the wilderness near where Mickey and Alan had fled. And it would be fairly easy to find out the schedule. Very few trains actually go by. Then he could guess where they might get off. Probably at a town. Probably the first time it stops. Probably in daylight. Not a foolproof plan by any stretch of the imagination, but perhaps a worthwhile gamble.

Mickey reasoned that Lorenzo might even know which city they were in, even though they themselves weren't sure. Perhaps he was nearby waiting. An old white van passed in the direction they were heading. It swerved to miss a pothole, thumped into yet another, and continued on without slowing.

With the sun rising big in the pale blue sky it threatened to be another scorcher. The stiffness in their aching limbs made it harder to walk along the roadside than it had been through the bush. Their clothes were ragged, dirty, and crisp, as though they had been saturated with starch.

Constantly Alan peeked over at Mickey. Every time he did his cheeks rose and the hint of dimples formed at the corners of his mouth.

"What?" she asked.

"Nothing," he said a little sheepishly, as though he had been caught at something.

"I'm a mess, all right, we already know that."

"No, well, yes, you're a mess. But you sure are gorgeous."

"Yeah, right," she replied sarcastically. She reached for her hair to pull it back from her face, but after stopping to look at her filthy hands she thought better of it.

Taking her hand in his once more, Alan said, "I don't know where we'll find somewhere to eat, but I'm starving. I vote we eat first."

"Great."

"But right after, we go straight to the police."

"Straight to the police," Mickey agreed.

They started walking. Alan tapped the back right pocket of his shorts, then the hip pocket on the other side, then both of the front pockets. "Umm," he began slowly, "I don't have my wallet. I must have lost it in the lake. I don't have any money, do you?"

"No." Mickey's shorts had no pockets. She kept everything in her knapsack, and that was still in the car.

"I've got the ring, we could hock it." She showed it to him.

Alan took her hand. "Is it real?"

"Yes."

"I don't know much about jewelry but it must be worth quite a bit."

Mickey nodded. "I guess so. It's a bit gaudy for my tastes. I don't wear jewelry. Max knew that. I think that's why he gave it to me. He's such a jerk. He wanted me to wear jewelry and fancy clothes."

"What's wrong with that?"

"It's not me." She gave her arms a flourish, then strode forward like a fashion model. "I prefer the casual look. She gave a little twirl and struck a haughty pose, head turned, chin resting on the rise of her shoulder. "Like this ensemble, I call it, *hommage à grunge.*"

Alan raved, *"Très chic, Mademoiselle."*

"Merci." Mickey nodded then frowned, and as she began to walk again she became sad and serious. "Actually this is what most people in São Paulo do wear. Rags."

On the corner there was a small restaurant with a gravel parking lot. Alan nodded toward it, then pointed at the phone booth in the parking lot. "No money," he said with a sigh. "Looks like the police win by default."

The operator connected them, the police agreed to have a cruiser come by and pick them up. While they waited Mickey impulsively called Max. She didn't have her calling card, but she knew the number.

There was a click. The ringing stopped. *"Olá."*

"Hello, Max Baerga please." She looked up at Alan.

"Como?" It was a woman's voice, young.

"Do you speak English?"

"Sim, sim, yes, little."

Mickey was surprised she didn't recognize the voice. She thought she knew all of Max's staff. Perhaps it was just the long phone lines, she thought. She listened carefully.

"I would like to speak to Max. *Señor Baerga, por favor.*"

At first there was no response. "Are you still there? Max Baerga, please."

"He no here. No here no more" was the answer.

"Where is he?" When the woman didn't respond Mickey tried some more Spanish. She understood a little Portuguese but couldn't speak it. *"¿Dónde está Señor Baerga? Señor Baerga?* Hello? Lorenzo Santos, *por favor?"*

The woman finally spoke but only uttered, "No."

"Louisa, Miranda?" The cook and the maid, she didn't know their last names.

"They no here."

"What is your name?"

"Como?"

"Your name? *¿Cómo se llama usted?"*

There was a pause before the woman responded, "Bridgitta Santos."

Mickey shrugged her shoulders. Lorenzo's sister perhaps. Same last name, but it's a common enough last name.

"When will Mr. Baerga be in? When? *Señor Baerga, cuando?*"

"He . . . He no here."

"Yes, but when will he be in again? *¿Cuando, Cuando?*"

"No, no. He no here, no more, no more."

"Where is Lorenzo?"

"No here, soon, soon."

"Soon?"

"Sim." The woman hung up.

Mickey turned to Alan. "She hung up, but she said Lorenzo will be back soon."

"How soon?"

"I don't know." She shrugged. "I had this idea maybe I could just talk to Max and somehow work things out."

"Great idea."

She shook her head. "Or maybe if Lorenzo had answered the phone . . . I could have just hung up and relaxed a bit. Somebody I never heard of answered the phone. And nobody I knew was there. Not Max, not even the cook or the maid."

"Is that strange?"

"Seems a little, I guess. And she said, 'Max—he

no here no more, no more.' Why did she say it that way? Was it just poor English? Has Max come to Canada too? But she said Lorenzo would be back soon. What does that mean?''

Chapter Five

They started eating the first chance they got—coffee, stale egg salad sandwiches, and fresh doughnuts—at the police station while they answered questions, asked questions, and made out reports. And, joy of joys, they managed to beg two hot soapy showers downstairs in the station house locker room. After that there was Chinese food in the food court at the mall, where they went and, with police collaboration, obtained a cash transfer from a branch of Alan's bank. They improved their wardrobe, replacing their rags with respectable clothes—cotton slacks, shirts, in fact, everything they would need until they got back to Mariposa. Once they had accomplished all their assorted chores they settled down for a wonderful dinner with red wine and Caesar salad, and fresh baked rolls.

Mickey had tender, juicy filet mignon wrapped in bacon, with fried onions, button cap mushrooms, asparagus tips, and baked potatoes with chives and sour cream, and then Cointreau, coffee, and a huge wedge of wild raspberry cheesecake. They indulged in their feast at a wonderful restaurant within sight of the train station while they waited for their ride back to Mariposa.

This time there would be no grimy flatbed under the stars; they had booked two sleeping cabins with soft mattresses and starchy white sheets. Even as she boarded the train with her new knapsack, Mickey was already luxuriating in her mind in the wondrous deep sleep to come, the crisp sheets, the soft pillow, and the gentle sway of the rail car. She felt wonderfully clean and wonderfully sated and tired, and finally safe. Constable Sinclair was certain they were safe, and wonderfully warm, basking in the glow of love she felt with Alan—this would be a sleep to revel in.

Their two compartments were across the narrow central hallway from each other. They each opened their doors and checked their respective little homes. The one seat, because of the late hour, was already folded down to make a bed. It virtually filled the tiny cubicle. There was enough space left over for a compact stainless-steel commode and for one person to stand. Smaller than a prison cell, it still looked like a sumptuous paradise. Mickey immediately sat on her bed and bounced a little and giggled in anticipation, then she lay back and stretched. Alan approached and she leaped up into his arms and hugged him. He shifted onto his heels. Mickey tightened her grip. Was it possible the barrier was back? "Alan," she murmured. What could it be? There was something holding him back. What? Didn't he love her? She had felt certain he did. Every moment in the wilderness had been endurable only because he was there—in fact, she had actually enjoyed the journey despite the deprivations. She enjoyed just being with him. Now he was so tentative. Why?

He kissed her on the forehead. She was so beautiful, he thought, so beautiful it caused a stab of pain. "Are you okay?" he asked, feeling uneasy, not wanting to leave, but afraid to stay any longer.

"Yes, wonderful. Are you?"

"Yes, of course." He kissed her on the cheek, then hesitated and drew back. "Well, you're exhausted. I'll see you in the morning." He stood in the doorway. "Good night."

What is wrong? He was suddenly acting again as if he were afraid of her. Did he still consider her only a friend? In her mind she had raced forward into romance. In her own mind she was already thinking of Mariposa as home, and . . . Was she mistaken? Mickey sunk to the bed.

"Lock the door behind me," he said. "Just in case the police are wrong."

Mickey responded, "I will, I have to brush my teeth

anyway.'' She closed her eyes and lay back, falling deeply into drowsy, dreamy thought—could she be wrong? How had that strange, tingling force field returned? Where did it come from?

Or was she the one that built the barrier? She felt so electrified when he was near. . . . Was her attraction to him so intense that she became a bit afraid? How could she be afraid of Alan? No one was kinder or gentler, or more understanding, but no one did she love so deeply. Was it fear of rejection? In her heart she was certain he loved her, there would be no rejection, and yet . . .

Alan too was exhausted; he didn't think he could sleep until the train was under way. The Royal Canadian Mounted Police constable was convinced Lorenzo was no longer a threat. They were trying to locate him. They had notified the Ontario Provincial Police detachment in Mariposa to check the cottage and to be on the lookout. They were checking with customs and immigration, and with authorities in Brazil. But they had never got a handle on what was going on, they never really understood the situation—who did? Alan mused. And they had assumed when Bridgitta had said ''soon,'' that that meant Lorenzo was on his way to Brazil. Soon could mean anything, especially to someone unfamiliar with the English language.

They'd underestimated Lorenzo before. Sure, Lorenzo hadn't been seen since he shot at them while they swam. That was hundreds of miles away in the

Northern Ontario bush. Perhaps the death of Sam had convinced Lorenzo that the chase wasn't worth it. Perhaps they'd never know why Sam and Lorenzo had been so determined to catch Mickey. Perhaps Lorenzo was somewhere nearby, biding his time, waiting for the perfect moment.

Alan was anxious. He needed a definite conclusion to the situation before he could relax. He walked the length of the car and stood at the entrance, then he stepped out onto the platform. He knew he'd feel better once the train started moving. It wasn't easy to jump aboard a moving train—he knew that firsthand—and passenger trains went much faster than freights. Stepping down the iron steps, he looked the length of the shiny silver-and-yellow passenger cars. The clean, soft berth was appealing but not as pleasant as the rough blustery flatbed under the stars with Mickey snuggled close. He had a lot to think about.

He wandered into the heart of the station where there was a coffee shop and a couple of small kiosks. It was a long trip, he considered. Tomorrow it'd be nice to laze about with Mickey reading the paper, watching the Canadian Shield rush by. He added a couple of snacks, trying to recall which were Mickey's favorites, and a couple of magazines. Yes, sitting up in the dome car with Mickey would be wonderful; every moment being with Mickey was nice. It always had been. He handed the cashier a ten-dollar bill.

Over the public address system he heard last call

announced, Sudbury, Parry Sound, Mariposa, Barrie, Toronto. The cashier gave him his change and he grabbed the two plastic bags.

A furtive movement captured his eye and Alan found himself staring at a vacant length of wall, a corner near the opening to a corridor. At first, as Alan slipped the change into his slacks pocket, he didn't know why he had suddenly looked up. Then he wondered and slowly recalled the shadowy movement, replaying it in his mind and trying to reconstruct exactly what he had seen. Someone had been there, staring at him. Someone had suddenly fled. Alan jogged forward. Now he could look down the length of the corridor. No one was there. He tried to fix the image in his mind. He was tired and it was difficult for his memory to cooperate. Whoever it was—he was certain he had seen someone—he was wearing a light-colored suit, maybe linen. Not that that meant anything, Alan thought. Lorenzo could be wearing anything by now. He pictured Lorenzo in his mind, remembered watching him move outside the car. No, Alan decided with relief, the man wasn't Lorenzo, this man had been large, and although he had moved quickly and surreptitiously, it was without grace.

He heard the gush of the air brakes being released. He'd better hurry. He started jogging down the corridor. Wheels started to grind. He hadn't realized how far into the station he had wandered. He began to run.

There was the train, moving, starting to pull out of

the station. Alan saw another man dart swiftly along the platform and leap aboard. The man hesitated on the iron step and looked back at Alan. Then he drew himself into the door but still stared back through the window. A small man with fluid, catlike movements, he wore jeans and a black nylon jacket, and he carried nothing.

Lorenzo? Alan dropped his bags. His open hands became fists, his arms were pistons. He was running frantically along the crowded platform, trying to dodge the people in the way. Slowly he was gaining on the train: running as fast as he could. The rear of the last car passed twenty feet in front. He was close. A bit closer and he could jump aboard, but it was accelerating. He willed himself to run faster. At the end of the station he was forced to jump down onto the tracks. Someone yelled for him to stop. Alan kept running. It was leaving him behind. The train was too far ahead and gaining speed.

Chapter Six

At the police station it was a different officer that met with Alan. Sergeant O'Keefe was tall and gaunt, with a gray, stony face, hollow cheeks and intense eyes: dark and rigidly steady. He sat behind his desk and listened to Alan's pleas calmly; he was unmoved but not without compassion. He gave the impression of a man who cared, but who had heard it all before. "I can't do that," he said simply.

"You have to," Alan continued. It was frustrating sitting, so he started to stand, then caught himself and sat again as he spoke. "She is alone, on that train, with someone who wants to kill her."

O'Keefe barely moved. "You yourself said you weren't sure if it was this Lorenzo fellow. I can't stop the Trans Canada in the middle of the bush, in the

120

middle of the night, and wake up every passenger and have every cabin, berth, and closet searched. Even if I wanted to there are not enough officers available to do such a procedure properly, not until the train gets to Sudbury.''

"That will be too late.''

"Perhaps, and like I said I am going to do everything possible to help you. Your story is a bit . . .'' O'Keefe glanced back down at the computer monitor. "Let me review it again. This fellow Max Baerga, from Brazil, is madly in love with your girlfriend, so he sends two thugs after her, who try to kill her. Why? And these two hardened professionals are thwarted by you and Ms. Chapeskie.'' He mulled that over for a moment, or, more accurately, allowed Alan a moment to reconsider it. "Sinclair, the constable you spoke with earlier today, has been very thorough. He has done everything possible.''

Alan squirmed in his seat. This wasn't helping Mickey. He had to do something. Someone had to do something.

O'Keefe tapped the Enter key. "So far, we haven't found your car, we haven't found any sign of the two perpetrators. Toronto customs did a search and they show that seventy-three Brazilians passed through Pearson International Airport the day Ms. Chapeskie arrived. No one named Sam. One named Lorenzo, but he was seven years old.''

"They could be using false passports.''

"Of course. We realize that. And who knows whether the passports were Brazilian or not. But this is what I am trying to show you, we are thorough. With computers we've checked thousands of possibilities. We've eliminated women and children and old people, and groups traveling together, like couples, families, and tour groups. We've eliminated people who have since left the country. It whittles the list down to eleven names, none of whom match the descriptions given. So—"

"But—"

"So," Sergeant O'Keefe interrupted with calm yet resolute authority, "it's most likely your Lorenzo has left the country." His penetrating eyes swung back to the computer monitor. "There are three possible suspects who roughly match the description; they arrived when you said, and have since departed. One in fact left from Winnipeg enroute to Los Angeles. This tallies with the phone call Ms. Chapeskie made to São Paulo and the woman saying Mr. Santos will be back soon. We've checked car rental records for large white Chryslers obtained with international driving licenses, nothing yet, but small independent rental places are difficult to check—no incidents of stolen white Chryslers either, and the Ontario Provincial Police have no reports of suspicious people asking questions in Mariposa or Sandhurst or along the Trans Canada highway, nothing. They are also looking in the area near Longlac for broken sumac bushes, and a car and a body in the bottom of a lake, nothing yet, but that will be a tough one, it will take awhile, but we'll find it.''

''Listen, she still could be on the train with Lorenzo, someone who wants to murder her.''

''I don't think so.''

''I just feel it. We are constantly underestimating him. I just know it was him.''

O'Keefe stared at Alan.

Alan continued, ''Get me back on the train.''

''Physically impossible.''

Now Alan stood. ''We have to do something.''

''Of course, we will do everything we can.'' The stare of the Royal Canadian Mounted Police sergeant caused Alan to sink back into his chair.

O'Keefe shifted his eyes back to the computer terminal. ''There seems to be a recent update added to this file, so let me finish.'' He hit the Enter key. His voice always maintained the same cool tone, but as he read his eyes opened a little wider. ''From a liaison officer in São Paulo we have learned Max Baerga has died.'' He looked up at Alan.

''Died?''

''Yes.''

''But how? When?'' Alan wondered what this could mean.

''It only says accidental, here, and a date of today. So, even if he was after Ms. Chapeskie, he is no longer. I'm sure this Lorenzo fellow has given up as well. It only stands to reason. Every indication is that he was one of the three Brazilians who arrived on the date in question and who have since departed Canada. Probably he phoned São Paulo for new instructions, found out Baerga had died, and decided to return. It all fits together very nicely. What's the point in pursuing Ms. Chapeskie, if Mr. Baerga is dead?''

What was the point in the first place? Alan wondered. And now that Max was dead. . . . ''But how can we be sure?'' he persisted.

''What I will do is alert the train staff about the situation. I will have them tell Ms. Chapeskie where you are and what you think you might have seen, and instruct them to keep an eye on her. I will arrange for a constable to board the train at Sioux Lookout and watch over Ms. Chapeskie. He'll use your cabin and ride all the way to Sudbury. If you hurry you might be able to make flight connections and meet the train, let's see. . . . I think you are too late to catch them in Sudbury, but tomorrow in Mariposa is certainly doable.''

The sergeant stood, implying that the meeting was drawing to a close. ''I think I'm being more than prudent here, don't you? I fully sympathize with you but the train is already a hundred miles into the bush. It's already night. It would be chaos trying to thoroughly search a train now; there isn't enough manpower available to do the job properly even if we wanted to. I trust you understand that. In just under three hours the

Trans Canada will be in Sioux Lookout. Once there, I'll get a constable on board.''

Somehow Alan wanted to do more.

''She keeps her door locked, she should be okay even if this Lorenzo Santos is somehow there. You can't break into one of those cabins without making a ruckus. From what you've said of this Lorenzo fellow he likes to do his dirty work discreetly, when there is no one around. There are plenty of people on the train, and soon there will be an RCMP constable. So, you try to take it easy and let us do our job.''

The last thing Mickey remembered before drifting off to sleep was, don't forget to brush your teeth and be sure to lock the cabin door—just in case. Be sure to lock the cabin door. . . .

Chapter Seven

The shade on her window was up. A blue darkness streamed in that dimmed and flickered like an old movie as the train curved and twisted past high ridges and tall trees.

Mickey considered the merits of getting out of the cozy bed and visiting the tiny commode. Her mouth was parched. Gazing at the door of her little cabin, she thought of Alan. First she wondered if he was awake, then she began a lazy drift through the things he had said and done, the time they had spent together, remembering the events of the last two days and sporadically skipping back to moments long ago when they were both children.

Quietly he saves my life, again and again, and asks for nothing in return, seems embarrassed when I thank him, or say I'm sorry, she considered. *Patiently he gets me out of dangerous predicaments. He doesn't complain when I destroy his tranquil life—he says he's happy just to be with me. A wonderful friend, and I can't question his friendship, or the great value a trusted friend is, but . . . somehow I thought we were progressing beyond that, somehow I had already, in my mind, progressed beyond friendship. Always he seems to be holding back. Is love for some reason out of the question? Could he be married—there was no sign of a wife at the cottage—maybe separated. Maybe engaged. Maybe he sees me as only a friend. . . . Could it be?* Could she be so wrong?

There was only one thing to do. First chance she got she was going to tell him she loved him, and not just as a friend. Suddenly she grinned. *I'll ask him to marry me! That'll put the fat in the fire.*

One last stretch was interrupted by a sudden giggle as she tried to envision his face: *Alan, will you marry me?* He'd be shocked; what would he do? He'd blush a little, he'd stammer a little and do that funny, shocked, shy, and awkward routine he has perfected—then what would he do?

Her mouth felt awful, as if her teeth were wearing woolly sweaters. *I should get up and get a drink.* It would be nice to get out of some of these clothes; she still wore her slacks and shirt. *And I can brush my teeth,* she thought, running her tongue around the inside of her mouth. She looked over at the door and suddenly she had energy to spare. *I just conked out, I never brushed my teeth, I never locked the door.*

Leaping to her feet, she took two quick steps, reached the door, and activated the door lock. She chided herself for forgetting. Lorenzo or not, she shouldn't be leaving her cabin door unlocked.

Another step and she was at the tiny sink. Everything was smooth and stainless steel. She grabbed her little knapsack, found her toothbrush, and peeled off the wrapper. She twisted on the water faucet, dampened her toothpaste, and just as she began to brush she heard a knock.

"Alan, just a second," she mumbled.

Still brushing her teeth, she moved to the door, reaching for the handle she had just locked, and then hesitated before turning. "Alan? Is that you?"

Stopping her brushing, she listened. He would answer, wouldn't he? Of course, in fact, anyone here on legitimate business would answer.

She stared at the door. Who was it? It couldn't be Lorenzo. She tried to resist jumping to conclusions, after all, had she even heard a knock? She knelt down, ear against the door. Was someone out there? Could it be Lorenzo? Until he was somehow apprehended her life could never be normal. Every unexpected noise would leave her shaking with terror, looking for places to hide and ways to fight back.

Her hand still held the door handle. The toothbrush was tossed into the little sink. She began to turn the lever. She was going to open it. She caught her breath. If she hadn't heard a knock then there was no danger in opening the door, if she had heard a knock, then she must warn Alan. Either way she must open the door. If Lorenzo was there she would scream so loudly they'd hear her for miles, train noise or not. She almost hoped Lorenzo would be there—this constant terror had to end. As the door opened through a narrow slit she could see a sliver of the dimly lit corridor, empty. She opened the door wider. She peeked each way. There was no one there. But it was difficult to see far. The passageway was not straight. In the middle of a "Chateau" car (hers was called Chateau Montebello) there were large bedrooms that caused the corridor to take a detour from the center to one side. You couldn't see very far, and that was disconcerting. She decided she would walk the length of the car but as she moved out into the corridor she noticed Alan's door was ajar.

She crept forward. It was dark, and the racing train was strangely still and quiet. "Alan," she called, first in a whisper, then a little louder. "Alan." With dread rising into her throat Mickey nudged his cabin door. The bed was still made, his knapsack rested on the middle—she could see that—but she couldn't see Alan. Opening the door wide she braced herself, prepared to fight, scream, or flee. Alan wasn't there—she could see the entire cabin in an instant, she knew he wasn't there, but it took much longer to comprehend.

In fact, it looked as if he had only been there long enough to drop his new knapsack. She felt a cold shudder. Where could he be? He wasn't on board; she was alone, she was sure of it.

Mickey ran the three short steps back into her cabin and locked her door. It gave her time to think, but she didn't—there was nothing to think about, she must find Alan or find out what had happened. So she flung open her door, this time loud and recklessly. Anger boiling over, she sprinted down the corridor, expecting at any moment to run into someone. Nothing could surprise her, she was prepared to meet anyone. But as she rounded each corner, she was confronted only by emptiness. She ran the length of another manor car and she still had not met anyone, not until she burst into the next car, an open coach. Rows of people sat dozing in their chairs. Swiftly she carried on, looking at every sleepy face that turned up toward her. In the lounge car several people were still milling about, imbibing and watching the rugged landscape glowing in the moonlight.

From beside her appeared a conductor. He was smiling benignly. Middle-aged, well groomed, he wore a plain blue suit; the only thing that identified him as a conductor were the initials VIA embroidered on the chest pocket. "Ms. Chapeskie?"

"Yes, I can't find—"

He interrupted her. "We have a message from a Mr.

Alan Mason. He got off the train in Winnipeg and he will meet you in Mariposa—''

''Is he all right?''

''As far as I know. And I was asked to tell you a fellow by the name of Lorenzo Santos may be on board.'' ''What?'' Mickey gasped. Got off in Winnipeg? He had only got on.

The congenial conductor started to tell her again, but she interrupted. ''Why did he—''

''I'm sorry, that's all I was told. The police called about an hour ago.''

Mickey was stunned. Alan got off, Lorenzo may be on board—why? How? What should she do now?

''Did you . . .'' She announced the thoughts as they sprang to mind. ''Did you knock on my door a few minutes ago?''

''I checked by about a half an hour earlier, but I didn't knock. It sounded like you were asleep. I didn't want to wake you.''

Mickey shifted onto her heels and quickly scanned the faces in the lounge. ''Have you seen a small, dark-skinned man on board? Mr. Santos? He'd be alone.''

''No, I don't believe so.''

Was that good? she wondered. ''And that's it? There is nothing else you can tell me?''

He shrugged. ''That's all I was told.''

Mickey's first thought was to run back to her cabin and lock the door, but the lounge area is part of the ''Park'' car, which was quite busy. Part of the car was a second-level observation area under a dome of glass. If she stayed there in company with several other travelers she'd be safe, she decided. Probably safer than being alone in her cabin. So, after thinking a moment, she settled into an empty seat near a young couple and a party comprising three older women and two men, all well into their late sixties or seventies. There she watched and listened to the people, always apprehensive, always anticipating some clue that something was amiss. Gradually she relaxed. Eventually she drifted off into a fitful, uneasy sleep.

When she awoke, not much later, still tired and groggy, the train was beginning to chug out of the small Sioux Lookout station. A young man, apparently a native Canadian, took the seat beside. As he made eye contact with her he reached inside the breast pocket of his charcoal gray suit jacket and took out a small wallet.

"I'm Constable Smoke with the RCMP," he said, showing her the badge inside. "If it's okay with you, I'll ride along here till you reach Mariposa."

"Okay? It's terrific."

Afterward he reassured her that Alan was safe and sound, and told how he had come to miss the train's departure in Winnipeg. Mickey continued the conversation, telling the constable about Lorenzo; she gave him a detailed description and told him about the knock on the cabin door that she was fairly certain she had heard.

"Well, you are safe now."

Mickey was less sure.

"We can stay here, or you can return to your roomette if you'd be more comfortable there. I could continue surveillance there just as easily."

"No, I don't think I want to be alone."

"Okay." He had a *Globe & Mail* newspaper in his lap. "I picked up a paper, if you are interested."

"Not right now, thanks."

Chapter Eight

The train began to slow as it passed through the Atherley Narrows. On the north side there was a short, marshy river, choked with weeds and bulrushes, a marina with corrugated steel roofing, and the tip of Lake Couchiching; on the south, the highway bridge, more marinas, and a wide expanse of the much larger lake, Lake Simcoe. One small sailboat leisurely circled, waiting for the train to pass and the bridge to reopen.

Bag in hand, Mickey stood first at the doors, eager to spy Alan and leap into his strong arms, hug him and soar into a delicious kiss like neither of them had ever even imagined could be possible. A kiss that would permanently clarify the ambiguity in their relationship. A kiss that would melt his shoes.

The train continued to slow. Constable Smoke stood

behind her. He had proven to be an amiable traveling companion while still maintaining his professional reserve. Mickey and Constable Smoke had breakfast in the dining car together, discussing among other things a small advertisement she had found in the back pages of his two-day-old newspaper.

The train did finally stop. Rather than leap she fell into Alan's arms and squeezed, relieved to find it felt so good and right. Arching her back, she turned her face to gaze up at him. Then, straining onto her toes, she reached his lips with hers.

It was crowded. And they stood between the main door of the train and the entrance to the small station. A child screamed. A young couple laden with suitcases accidentally jostled Mickey from behind. Constable Smoke waited respectfully in the background.

Mickey brought her lips to brush against Alan's, but each settled only for an instant before his scuttled off to rest briefly in the corner of her mouth.

"I've missed you," he said, steering her out of the churning passenger flow.

"Me too, it's only been a few hours, but—"

"Feels like years."

"Yes," she said falteringly. Her determination withered; there were so many people and the dusty noisy station was hot, impersonal, and distracting. Maybe this wasn't the right time. Maybe tonight, alone, at the cottage—tonight would be perfect. No distractions. She'd make a lovely dinner. She remembered the moonlight dancing on the water, the deck glowing, the cool silence. She hated putting the moment off but tonight would be better. And today there was so much to do!

"Oh, Alan," she said and gasped, remembering her guardian. "This is Constable Smoke."

Alan voiced his appreciation and shook hands. When the young man took his leave, Mickey pulled two neatly folded pages from her knapsack. "Can I get this typed up somewhere, do you think? Really fast?"

"Sure, how fast?" Alan took the two papers from her. He kept walking toward his car.

"Half an hour?" She had borrowed a pen and paper from the conductor.

"Half an hour." He laughed. "I guess so, but why? What is it?"

"A résumé." She showed him the scrap of newspaper she had ripped out.

"You work fast." He was reading the advertisement. "Just outside Mariposa," he murmured as pleasure burst brightly into his face.

She checked her watch. "I have less than an hour, and I need new clothes, and I should get my hair cut. It's at a new private school, opening this fall, Simcoe College. I'm not sure where exactly it is, or how far . . . if we can't make it . . ."

"Plenty of time," he said, and rolled his eyes.

"Today is the last day—"

"I'll drop you downtown. I've picked up another car." He nodded toward another shiny new Cavalier, this one a bronze color. "Then I'll get Glenda at the copy shop to type this up. She does a nice a job with résumés. You can pick out some clothes and you should be able to get your hair done. Tell Ginny at Hair Today that I sent you, and I'll be forever in her debt if she can do you quick. Okay? So let's get going."

Mariposa was small enough that anywhere was nearby. On the short drive to Leacock Street Alan barely had enough time to recap recent developments with Mickey. He told her about Max's death; he'd been found on the beach near Rio de Janiero, yesterday morning, three days after she had fled his mansion.

"Drowned?"

"Yes," Alan confirmed. "That's what they say."

Mickey was a little surprised. "He was a strong swimmer."

"Good swimmers do drown."

"Yes, of course. And he did go to that beach fairly often. He kept a boat at a nearby marina. It all fits."

Alan quickly repeated the findings of the RCMP, explaining how they had arrived at the conclusion that Lorenzo had left.

"So we are finally rid of Lorenzo."

"Hopefully." Alan nodded, but not too convincingly.

He stopped the car in front of a NO PARKING sign on the side of the main street. "I'm not an expert on ladies' clothing stores, but I think your two best bets are just up, about a dozen doors. Hair Today is right here. You should probably nip in and check with Ginny first, then shop. If you have any problems with anyone, mention my name, it probably won't help but you never know."

"Okay," Mickey said as she opened the door.

"I'll be back in thirty minutes."

"Thanks a lot, Alan."

"My pleasure."

From there the day went like clockwork: clothes, hair, résumé. She was transformed into a new woman, a professional woman. Impeccably groomed and attired in a polished silk suit jacket and skirt, taupe, over a plain crew neck blouse in light cream, she was almost ready. The short drive out to the college grounds provided Mickey with the last ingredient she needed to present herself to best advantage, an opportunity to relax and gather her wits.

Chapter Nine

 $\mathbf{B}$ y late afternoon the pleasant weather gave way to
more vigorous conditions. On Lake Couchiching a
stiff breeze built up a fierce chop. In front of the cottage, waves bashed into the rocky shore and suddenly
burst skyward. Huge water droplets whipped by the
wind splattered against the cottage windows and siding, and plopped along the deck like a faltering rain.
Mickey stood at the sink, washing dishes, putting them
up on the wooden drying rack, and staring out the
front window at the lake.

The cottage was a rectangle, with the large cedar
deck on two sides, running the width of the front and
a little farther to enable a narrow slice to run along
the outside of the kitchen. That's where the door most
frequently used was located. It opened directly into the

kitchen, with a small powder room on the left. The
kitchen was large with a long, L-shaped counter running under the windows. Also facing the deck and the
lake, at the other front corner, was the master bedroom. Wedged between the kitchen and the bedroom
there was a dining area with an old round table. The
dining area had the only other entrance, a sliding glass
door situated in the middle of two large windows. The
center of the cottage was an open living area with a
cathedral ceiling and dominated by a wide stone fireplace along the rear wall. The remaining two corners,
the ones closest to the back lane and the driveway,
had two small bedrooms. The second washroom, the
much larger one, was nestled between the master bedroom and one of the small bedrooms. All these rooms,
the bedrooms, and the main washroom opened off the
living room, chalet style. There were no hallways in
the entire building. The big main room, in the center,
had four sofas in a square surrounding a large square
coffee table, sort of a conversation pit that required
living-room traffic to flow around.

Mickey dried the last plate and put it away. She
glanced at the clock over the door. There was still at
least an hour before Alan said he would be home from
work. Taking the tray of lasagne off the counter, she
slid it into the preheated oven. Then she went to the
fridge and pulled out every vegetable she could find.
Thumping the base of the head of iceberg lettuce on

the cutting board, she wriggled out the core, then began ripping the lettuce and dropping it into a colander.

"Mickey this is your home, you can stay as long
as you want": he had said it the first night, she remembered. She thought of it many times, she knew he
meant it, but was it true? She could hardly just stay
as a friend; that would be impossible—not as a
friend—even if she got the teaching job.

The job prospects were surprisingly good. The
school president explained they were looking for a
wide range of teachers, young and old, male and female, some with vast experience, some quite new to
the profession, to provide continuity, breadth, vitality,
and color to the school. He specifically wanted inter-
esting people with energy, a zest for knowledge, and
a solid academic background. Her hard work and super grades might just pay off, Mickey considered. The
school's motto was to be "a passion for life and learn-
ing." He was thrilled she had gone to Pepperdine University in California, and that she was originally from
the Toronto–Mariposa area. They even discussed the
possibility of Mickey organizing school trips to the
Mayan ruins on the Yucután peninsula, maybe arrang-
ing to help on an archaeological dig. They already had
under contract for the history department the quintes-
sential stereotype, an eccentric old English gentle-
man—tweed jacket, pipe, and cane—with impeccable
credentials and extraordinary experience, and (she remembered the school president's words precisely)

"possibly a vivacious young female with a fresh perspective would balance things nicely."

It was exciting; she tried not to get her hopes too high but her life felt like it was about to burst forth in riotous blossom. In less than a week everything had completely changed, thanks largely to Alan.

One piece of the puzzle remained, and it was the most puzzling piece of all. Deep in her soul she knew she loved Alan, and was certain he loved her. All that was needed was that one moment when it could all break out into the open. Somehow they managed to constantly skirt the edges of that moment without it ever actually occurring. Something always managed to get in the way and hold them back. She was convinced now it was as much her fault as his. Doubtless she exuded the same heightened aura that pulled him close yet held him away, doubtless it caused him as much confusion as it caused her. But that would all change tonight.

"Alan, will you marry me?" She practiced saying the words out loud. "Alan, I love you, let's get married." No, the question Will you marry me? sounded nicer. What she really wanted to hear was "Mickey, I love you, will you marry me?" She was an independent, liberated woman; she'd asked men out on dates before, and though it seemed a trifle sexist, she admitted to herself even as she thought it, a marriage proposal sounded nicer coming from a man.

Somehow, some way, tonight it would work out.

Tonight would be perfect, there would be no distractions. Just the two of them alone in the cozy cottage. If the wind continued to puff up, well, there was wood in the fireplace, they could have a little fire if they wanted. Tonight was the night.

She was humming when the phone rang. Putting down the knife and using the last spiral-cut radish to complete the ring adorning the salad in the crystal bowl, Mickey crossed into the living room.

"Hi," Alan said. "You got home okay?"

"Yes, I splurged on a cab."

"Must have cost a fortune from out there in the boonies."

"Yes, it did. But it was a special occasion."

"That sounds promising. The interview went well?"

"Super, but I won't know anything for a few days at least."

"I hope you don't mind, but the Kirklands are coming up this weekend, remember, Jim?"

"Sure."

"He's married. His wife is Sandy, you'll like her. And I wouldn't be surprised if more of the old gang drop in. Now that Jim knows, word about you will spread pretty quick. In fact, I've got a message here that Dan Lauder phoned, but I keep missing him. So who knows what's in store for the weekend."

"We'll have tonight alone though?"

"Yes."

"That's good. We certainly have a lot to talk about," Mickey added.

"Yes, we do. I'm swamped with work here, but I can't concentrate right now, so I'm leaving early anyway. I'll be about ten minutes."

"Terrific, I'll have supper ready."

"Really? I was going to pick up something."

"No, don't. It's all done."

"You don't need anything?"

"Just you," Mickey announced with an excited giggle that only he could elicit.

"Hmm, I can hardly wait."

"For supper?"

"Yes, for supper . . . no, not supper . . . well, both."

She knew he was blushing. "Both," Mickey questioned. "Both, what?"

"You know, supper and . . . you."

"Ah, I see," she said. "I hope I don't let you down."

"Impossible. Look, if I don't hang up I'll never get home, and I am really, really looking forward to getting home, so . . ."

After slow good-byes Mickey replaced the receiver.

A lot to talk about, she pondered. And a lot to do, ten minutes! The salad, the garlic bread, the lasagne, where to begin? She knew Alan wouldn't mind if supper wasn't completely prepared, but she would. She didn't want any distractions once he got home, just relaxation and conversation. Tonight was going to be absolutely perfect. It would be the most memorable night of her life, she could feel it.

First she reached into the hot oven and peeled the aluminium foil back off of the lasagne. A gust of hot, humid air swept up into her face. It smelled fabulous. She may not be the cook her mom was but she knew she wasn't bad. Already hot and bubbling, the lasagne would be ready in time. She liked it a little crispy on top, and if memory served, so did Alan, so she left the foil off. Next she took the French loaf she had bought, sliced it right down the middle, and laid it on a cookie sheet. Using a press, she squeezed two cloves of garlic into a bowl of soft butter, added a sprinkle of tarragon, and mixed it around before slathering it on the bread. Then she slid the sheet into the oven. Hanging on a hook in the big cedar rafters—just where her mother used to keep them, as combination ornament and ac- coutrement—she found a familiar wicker basket and took it down and spread a cloth napkin in it.

All the time she listened keenly for the sound of a car, or a car door, or a step on the deck, or the click of the screen door in the kitchen. A temporary letup in the fluctuating breeze allowed the sounds of a car engine to filter through to her. *He's here!*

The salad still wasn't finished. Hastily she chopped chunks of tomato and golden peppers. She mixed them together with black olives; using her fingers, she sprin- kled them into the middle of the salad. The salad dressing was given a shake. She opened the cruet and allowed a drop to fall on her finger which she tasted by wiping her finger on her tongue. After checking the bread she took the salad and the dressing to the table.

Matches she got from a beer stein on the fireplace mantel exactly where her dad used to keep them; she raised the delicate glass chimneys and lit both candles. Standing back, she examined her handiwork and was happy with what she saw: elegant but not pretentious, friendly, cozy, comfortable, almost perfect.

In the middle of the table there was a bouquet—not roses, roses would have been nice, but perhaps the wildflowers she had picked—blue chicory, white Queen Anne's lace, daisies, and black-eyed Susans—were more apropos.

She glanced toward the door, but still no Alan, not even the sound of footsteps.

The corkscrew was already twisted into the bottle of red wine. She picked it up and drew out the cork. She filled his glass and hers, then took a little sip.

What could be taking him so long?

Crossing into the kitchen, she opened the door and leaned out into the breeze. No car could be seen in the driveway. She walked back along the side deck until she could see the entire backyard. There was no one there. Perhaps she'd been hearing things.

Back inside she hesitated over the oven before pulling out the garlic bread. The butter was melted; it was almost ready. She poked it, wondering whether to leave it in—he must be here soon, or leave it out. She really didn't want it to be all dried out and dusty. She left it on the top of the stove.

Her father had been notorious for getting wrapped up in something at the office and not getting away as planned. Perhaps Alan was the same way.

If he didn't hurry he'd miss the last of the sunset, she thought as she picked up the phone again. She was halfway through the number when she realized there had been no dial tone. Flicking the plunger accomplished nothing. Probably just the wind had blown down a telephone pole—Lake Couchiching, she mused, from the Ojibway language, meaning "lake of many winds." Will it still be windy this weekend? How many people will come? How many will she know? It'd been years since she'd been waterskiing; the thoughts just flitted through her mind. Waterskiing again would be great fun, as long as she hadn't forgotten how.

Picking up her glass of wine, Mickey walked to the kitchen window and stared at the last glimmer of the sunset. Black clouds were beginning to creep over the lake.

One thing the cottage lacked was a cozy chair where you could sit and stare out over the water, she conceded. On good days you could always sit outside. But there was an awful lot of inclement weather. It'd be nice to have a little corner with a window and a big stuffed chair to sit and watch the sunset and the snow fall. She wondered if a little addition could be tacked on somewhere. Mickey leaned against the counter.

Surely ten minutes had passed, more like twenty or thirty. The candles were down at least an inch. Was she just being anxious? Alan, she recalled, was chronically punctual; she'd never known him to be late.

Taking a quick peek out of her rear bedroom window, she saw that his car was there.

Racing back to the kitchen, she slid the bread back into the oven. Out came the lasagne, crispy on top, just right. With a long knife she began to cut out squares.

The bread would take another minute or two, but otherwise everything was ready. Now, what was taking him so long?

She had seen his car. She took the tray of lasagne to the table and laid it on the pad she had prepared for it.

There, finally, his step trod heavy on the deck— another step surprisingly clumsy. Despite the howl of the wind and the muffled crush of the distant waves, she could hear a slow awkward *clump, ka-lump*. His footsteps? It sounded peculiar, like Frankenstein. At first she smiled, wondering at his playfulness. What was he doing? Why tonight? She wanted tonight to be romantic, to settle the basic questions of their lives. Hadn't he implied the same thing on the phone—lots to talk about, he'd said it. It wasn't like him to be kibitzing, not now; surely he understood how important tonight was.

Clump. Ka-lump. The noise scared her.

Cocking her head to one side, straining to hear, she considered the possibilities and fought the strident demands of her impulses. Nimbly Mickey leaped from the kitchen and drew open the sliding glass door that led out to the front deck. The wind rushed in. A peal of deep thunder rumbled slowly across the heavens.

Chapter Ten

At the side of the cottage the screen door began to open, and the wind caught the edge, flinging it violently against the siding. Glass broke in long shards and fell crashing onto the wood. A moment passed before Alan stumbled in. He fell, bucking and twisting angrily. Landing hard on his knee and left shoulder, he kicked out with his legs, catching only air.

Lorenzo, gun in his left hand, slipped agilely to the center of the kitchen. As Alan struggled onto his knees, Lorenzo, primed in a crouch, took a quick survey of the scene; then, springing forward cat-quick, he stopped when he could see the curtains flapping and the open sliding glass door. Immediately he deduced what had occurred. Whirling about, he clubbed Alan down with the butt of his gun, then he kicked him once in the stomach before taking another nylon wire tie from his back pocket and tightly cinching Alan's feet together. Then he dashed to the door, pausing before stepping out gingerly yet swiftly into the wind.

Alan tried to catch his breath. The rag in his mouth made it difficult. He lay on his stomach, trying to think of what to do. He was relieved Mickey had got away. He'd been intentionally clumsy and heavy with his feet as he approached the kitchen door in the desperate hope that Mickey might somehow be alerted.

He started squirming across the floor. He felt the rush of the breeze roaring in the front door. If she had shut the door behind her, she'd have had more of a head start. Alan made it to the small table with the phone and knocked the phone down. If she had shut the door behind her, Lorenzo would waste time searching the cottage. She knew the area, she might have got away. She could still. He was relieved she might get away, and terrified that he hadn't had that one moment alone with her, just one more chance— somehow he had to find a way. Given one more chance he wouldn't waste it.

The sliding glass door slid closed with a thud. The buffeting wind eased. It was quieter. He heard the lock click into place. Frantically he tried to pound the telephone buttons 9, 1, 1 with his nose. It wasn't working, there was no sound at all.

Then he was grabbed again from behind.

''Alan.''

Up jerked his hands, then they fell, now completely loose and free.

"I was in the bedroom. I'm not running away again," Mickey muttered. "No way." She still held the big knife she had used to cut the lasagne.

Already he was reaching for the phone as she cut away his gag. He flicked the receiver several times.

"It's dead," she told him.

He checked the wire; it was still plugged in. Mickey cut the nylon tie that bound his ankles.

"It's been dead for a while," she said as she raced to the kitchen door. "I thought it was just the wind, but . . ." Slamming the door with a thud, she twisted the lock. The garlic bread was beginning to burn in the oven.

"Now what?" Alan asked. "This won't keep him out long."

"I know." She shrugged. Then her eyes sparkled. "I got us this far, now it's your turn."

"Thanks. When he sees the doors shut he'll know we're in here."

She had gone into the dark master bedroom and was peering into the night. "Maybe we should get out." Then she immediately contradicted herself. "I don't want to go back outside. He's out there somewhere."

She went to the far rear corner of the building, her old bedroom, and looked out the window. "If we knew where he was, it'd be different."

Alan was close behind. He gently touched her

shoulder and encouraged her to turn toward him. For a moment he held her upper arms in his hands, then let go. But his smooth, loving face edged closer.

"Mickey," he murmured. "I can't wait any longer."

His eyes sought a response.

Her voice fell soft and low like his, but her pulse raced. "Your timing is atrocious." Her throat suddenly went dry.

"I know, but it could be worse."

"How?" An impish smile swept through her face. She raised her head to him and tilted back slowly as he eased down. She could see the yearning love in his eyes. *Hurry,* she implored. But he wouldn't be rushed. Her eyes flickered closed.

Three bullets smashed into the lock of the wooden kitchen door. Lorenzo was outside the kitchen.

"Hide," Alan said with a gasp, and he pulled her down, but then as she sank to her knees he slipped away. She wanted to follow, but hesitated. Maybe it would be better to be apart. She moved under her bed. Give Lorenzo two enemies, two targets. Maybe one of them could get close. There was no choice, they couldn't run anymore, they had to fight. They had to battle him, outwit him, somehow capture him once and for all.

She slipped out from under the bed and squeezed into the corner behind the dresser. She had the knife in one hand. She picked up a shoe with the other; she wanted something, anything to use as a weapon. Squeezing another weapon gave her solace, even if a shoe was all she could find.

Lorenzo didn't burst in the side door. What would he do? Just come in shooting? What was he doing?

It would be better if the house was dark. Then maybe she could get close enough for the knife to be effective. She decided to leave her hiding spot, it wasn't much good anyway. Slipping into the living room, she turned off a table lamp. Several lights still burned, and the place was lit up like a circus, not very romantic—what had she been thinking?

Where was Alan? She didn't see him.

At the front, three more bullets smashed into the lock of the sliding-glass door.

Mickey dove between a sofa and the big square coffee table.

Then the house went completely dark, save for the two candles on the dining-room table.

She thought of hiding in the wood box near the fireplace. She'd hidden there before as a child. She squirmed a few feet toward it. But what good would hiding do? It would only prolong the inevitable. She tried to control her terror. Panic was an even worse threat than Lorenzo. If she panicked it was all over.

Would anybody hear the gunshots, she wondered— no, not likely. Again there was no one nearby. And the sound wouldn't carry, not with the wind and the waves. Tomorrow night was Friday, when all the cottages would be occupied. But tonight, they were on their own. Lorenzo had seized his opportunity wisely. They needed to be just as wise, and wiser. They needed a plan.

Where was Alan? He had pulled the main power switch, she suddenly realized. Darkness was their ally, not Lorenzo's. Surely, it was Alan who had pulled the lever. That meant he was in the small bathroom near the kitchen door—that's where the main fuse box was.

The candles flickered. The bullet holes caused enough of a breeze to fan them, but they couldn't be blown out because they were in loose glass chimneys.

Mickey considered going to put them out. But they were close to the sliding glass doors at the front. Any moment, she knew, Lorenzo would burst in. She edged forward. From where she cowered behind the side of the sofa she could now see both entrances. She could see the splintered wood of the side door, and the hole where the lock had been in the door that led to the front deck. Both doors were still closed. Lorenzo was still outside. He had shot out both locks so he could enter quickly and easily and they wouldn't know which door until he was there with his gun. That made sense; that was what he was doing, she decided.

He had fired six shots, but he had also taken plenty of time to reload and think. Counting his shots wouldn't help—she didn't know how many bullets his gun had. She tried to discover any advantage she could.

What would Lorenzo do? Once he had decided he wouldn't wait long. He wouldn't want to give her and Alan too much time to prepare. He might even assume they had a gun. He probably didn't know handguns were rare in Canada.

She had no idea what to do. Her mind raced but got nowhere. Their only chance was to be smart, she knew that, but how to be smart, how to outthink a fox, a fox with a gun. Their only advantage was that they out-numbered him two to one, that was something. And they knew the cottage intimately.

The side door burst open. But other than the wind returning to swirl around inside the cottage, nothing else happened. Think, Mickey!

The glass door opened. She thought she saw a shadow slip by. But no one entered. Inside curtains and papers began to fly about.

A movement—Lorenzo—filling the doorway and aiming his gun into the middle of the kitchen.

Mickey jumped up from where she hid. She stood in full view. She tossed her shoe at him and made herself an easy target.

Chapter Eleven

It was the first time she had ever seen Lorenzo surprised, but it only lasted for the instant it took their eyes to lock. He dodged the shoe easily, and already the gun was on the move. Now the barrel swung fast. Mickey twisted backward, landing on her toes, spinning and diving, falling on her back. The gun erupted once. She was on the floor and squirming deeper into the living room, into the shadows, beyond Lorenzo's sight.

He fired twice more, blindly into the wall behind where she lay, splintering the paneling. He dashed forward to the edge of the room.

She saw him coming to the corner. Behind a sofa she lay perfectly still, hoping it would take him a moment longer to find her. She squeezed the knife and held her breath. She could see his torso, jeans, and black nylon jacket, but not his legs. He fired twice more randomly into the dark corners. His head jerked to and fro.

A flurry of confused motion—something happened, but what? She could no longer see Lorenzo. It sounded as if he was on the floor struggling. The darkness erupted with two more sparks, gunshots ripping crazily into the ceiling. Alan!

Mickey jumped to her feet and ran to where the two bodies tangled. She prepared to hack down with the knife. But in the murky tumult it was impossible to know where to aim. There was another flash, another bang; without thinking she lunged at the gun. The knife hit bone. She saw the gun fall free, and she kicked it away. It was Lorenzo who swore and Alan who spun to his feet. She cocked the arm again. Lorenzo was writhing on the floor in pain. He screamed something she didn't comprehend.

Alan pushed the gun toward her. Mickey shifted the knife to her left hand and grabbed the gun and aimed it directly at Lorenzo. Her face was stern; she wanted no one to think she had any qualms about shooting him if she had to, because she didn't.

Firmly in charge, Alan extracted a bundle of cable ties from Lorenzo's back pocket.

"He's bleeding pretty bad," Mickey said. "We should get him a towel or something, and we better get him to the hospital."

"In a second. I don't trust him. I want him tied up first."

Alan took one arm and pulled it around Lorenzo's back, but just when it looked like they had him, he lashed out twisting and kicking. Alan thumped him in the back of the head, snatched the bleeding wrist and wrenched it high up Lorenzo's back. Still the enemy squirmed and whipped his legs out. Alan got a knee onto the Brazilian's back and kept yanking the arm. Lorenzo bit Alan on the calf and tried to roll and rise.

"A little cobra, isn't he?" It was a fourth voice, behind them. Astonished, both Alan and Mickey stopped, only turning to look. "He's creating a little diversion, I think. So you wouldn't notice me enter. Sly fellow. Now, Mickey, be a good lass and hand him back his gun."

It couldn't be. But it was. Sam. And Sam had a gun. He was close enough to touch Mickey, and the gun was pointed directly at her head.

She was stunned into silence and inaction. Lorenzo was on his feet; already he had his gun back from her.

"Did she bite you?" Sam asked.

Lorenzo paid no attention.

Sam continued with amusement, "Nasty bit of blood."

It was Lorenzo's turn to use the cable ties. Quickly he cinched up Alan's hands.

"I don't understand," Mickey burst out. "I've never understood. Why are you doing this? Is it the ring you want? That's the only thing I can think of. Is it worth all this? I don't want it. I never wanted the ring. It's on the dresser in the little bedroom. Just take it and leave us alone.''

Sam snorted.

Lorenzo ignored the hot sticky blood spewing from his wrist. He managed to tie Alan's ankles together. Alan didn't fight back, it would be fruitless; it would only provoke Sam to shoot them immediately. But not fighting—what hope did they have?

Mickey continued to shout. ''Well, what is it, then? You can't take me back to Max, Max is dead. Don't you know that? He drowned in the ocean. While you were chasing me. You can't take me back to him now.''

Lorenzo looked puzzled; he faltered and tossed a quick glance in Sam's direction. He had Alan tied securely: three cable ties, one on his ankles, another around his wrists with his arms around his back, and a third connecting the two together. Alan was on his stomach bent back like a bow.

''Phone, if you don't believe me. Phone São Paulo. They can tell you.''

Sam looked over at Lorenzo. They paused.

Mickey kept insisting as Lorenzo pushed her to the floor, ''I tell you he's dead. He's dead.'' Lorenzo cinched up her hands.

''This was all crazy from the beginning. I don't understand. You couldn't take me back there anyway, but now he's dead. What's the point?''

Neither Sam nor Lorenzo spoke. Quickly Lorenzo trussed up Mickey like he had Alan. Then he pushed them back to back and used the cable ties to attach them together.

''You are going to kill us, I want to know why. What difference does it make now? Tell me. Tell me why. I don't know why. I'd like to know why.''

''I guess they are still afraid of us. They aren't going to say anything,'' Alan said angrily.

''What are you doing?'' Mickey demanded, straining to twist and see her adversaries. But she couldn't find them. ''Why won't you say anything?''

''They've had their chance, they aren't going to tell us.''

Mickey shuddered. She swallowed tears. ''Oh, Alan, I'm so sorry.'' They were still back to back.

His hands unfolded and encompassed hers. He gave a gentle squeeze. ''I love you'' was all he said.

''I love you too,'' she answered, expecting to hear Sam interrupt with a snide comment. ''My coming here has been such a disaster for you.''

''Don't say that.''

''Why?''

''It's not true.''

''But . . . you can't say you are just happy to be with me,'' she whispered. She heard him smile. ''Alan, I wish I could see you.'' Then she screamed with angry exasperation and yanked at her bonds. She squirmed until she began to cry.

"Mickey, Mickey," Alan whispered. Her contortions had them side by side, on their stomachs. "Look! look!" He was insistent.

Opening her eyes, she saw where he was looking. The knife, still wet with blood. Together they squirmed forward. Why wasn't Sam or Lorenzo stopping them?

"Have they gone?" Mickey said with a grunt. "Where are they?"

"I don't see them."

Was it possible? Were they alone?

"Where have they gone?" she said gasping.

"I don't know. They've gone outside."

"Why?"

"I don't know. To get something. I don't know. Just get the knife."

"Yes."

It was on the floor beside her. Her hip brushed against it, but her hands, bound tightly, would not reach. "I can't."

"You have to." Alan rocked onto his side. "On three. One, two, three."

They rocked together and Mickey grasped the blade, holding it tight as they rocked back down to their stomachs.

"Got it," she announced.

"Okay, cut. Hurry."

"Just a second." She fumbled the knife around so she held the handle. Blindly she began to search with the knife, trying to catch any plastic binding. It was long and awkward. She began to cut.

"Is that it? Or is it you?"

"It's not me. Hurry, they'll be back."

Suddenly Mickey screamed, "Alan! The candle!"

During the tussle the tablecloth had been shifted askew. Plates and glasses had tumbled to the floor. One candle tottered on the edge of the big round table. The doors were still open. The breeze kept nibbling at the corners of the tablecloth, nudging the candle nearer the precipice. It wobbled, then hung in the air. It fell before either of them could react. Almost instantly the light tablecloth ignited. The flames sprinted to the curtains and started licking at the wood ceiling.

Chapter Twelve

"Cut," implored Alan, his voice calm but insistent. "Don't worry, just cut." There wasn't time to be careful. She slipped the knife around behind their backs, hunting, catching, and bursting free the bindings.

His hands sprang free. He grabbed the knife and in a moment they were both free.

The fire was spreading rapidly.

"We need water!" Mickey screamed.

Alan already had the fire extinguisher.

Fanned by the wind, the flames had skipped from curtain to curtain. The kitchen was ablaze. Mickey ran to the bathroom and turned on the tap. "I need a bucket."

The fire extinguisher was spurting out thick ribbons of foam. For a moment it looked like Alan was win-ning. Then the fire extinguisher fizzled out, empty. He dropped it and hesitated a moment, looking for her. It was hopeless. Already the roof was burning.

Mickey had a small plastic wastepaper basket filled with water; she ran out of the small powder room and tossed it into the flames, producing a sizzle but little effect. The fire was roaring. It crept along the wood floor and the big cedar beams in the ceiling. The cottage was all wood, old dry wood that burned eagerly.

Mickey started back to the bathroom. Alan stopped her. "It's too late."

"No."

"We have to get out."

"No!" Mickey screamed. "The cottage—" Her words were cut. Until he heard her outburst of coughing, he hadn't realized how acrid the air was becoming.

"We must leave!" Alan commanded. The worst of the fire had engulfed the only two doors, the only escape. Black smoke was clogging their lungs and making their eyes water.

"Alan, the cottage will burn down."

"Yes, but at least we won't." He swept her up into his arms. She didn't fight. Inside she knew he was right. The cottage was burning too quickly. The breeze was cheering on the flames, inspiring them to burn faster and faster, gobbling up the building and everything in it. It couldn't be saved.

Alan carried her, darting into the kitchen and out
the door. "It's too late."

"We can get buckets from the lake," Mickey muttered feebly.

"We don't have buckets, and even if we did, it's
far too late."

She slipped out of his arms and stood pressed
against him, hiding.

There was a sudden crash and the flames that had
flickered above the treetops came down to eye level
with the failure of the walls. In the bright firelight
stood the big stone fireplace. The fire was a great torch
that illuminated the entire property. There were no cars
in the driveway. There were no people to be seen.
Unless hidden deep within the far shadows, Sam and
Lorenzo had fled.

The heat was intense. Stepping forward, Alan
stooped and picked up a long white box; slowly he
handed it to her. "I wanted this evening to be so special, perfect."

"Me too."

She removed the lid from the box. Inside, nestled
in white tissue, was one perfect red rose. She was
speechless. Suddenly there was no howling wind or
waves crashing upon the rocks, no Sam, no Lorenzo,
no fire, only Alan's blue eyes, looking shy yet quietly
bold. Slowly but surely their lips drifted together.
"I've always loved you," Alan murmured, just before
their lips brushed.

Sweet, gentle, tentative, bursting with electric excitement, the kiss began, then grew deep and rich. Her hands slid up his arms, over the width of his shoulders. Her fingers caressed the nape of his neck, the other hand furrowed into his short thick hair. She got a good grip. He wasn't getting away, not this time, he wasn't getting away, not ever.

As Alan drank in the luxurious sensuality of all of Mickey, he thought to himself, *forever, forever.*

Alan shifted his weight to kick off his canvas shoes. They were hot and uncomfortable, it felt as if the soles had begun to melt while he was fighting the fire. The tall grass was cooler.

From the lane at the back of the cottage a raucous noise suddenly distracted them. The kiss finally broken, they turned to look, still entwined in each other's arms.

A siren. A wide fire engine pushed back the bushes on either side of the narrow drive. It dodged around the volleyball net and carried on across the lawn to the edge of the water. Men scrambled. One strode up to them in his heavy suit, visor up. "No one inside?" It was a question, a hopeful question.

"No." Alan shook his head.

The fireman looked relieved. "Good, because I don't think there is much we can save, other than keeping it from spreading."

Alan nodded. Mickey remained snug in the crook

of his arm, head on his shoulder, both hands holding him about the waist.

Before them, hoses were being unraveled; one ran to the lake, two more were pulled toward the fire, spewing water onto the flames. The resulting steam and black, charred timbers made the scene look even more devastating.

"Oh, Alan, the cottage . . ." Mickey was crying. She was crying for her parents. They had loved the cottage, and now it was destroyed.

"We can rebuild it."

"It won't be the same."

"No. Well, a lot of it can be, the deck, the geraniums, the big kitchen, but you're right, it won't be the same. Instead of the perfect summer cottage we'll make it the perfect home. Maybe make it a little bigger, a year-round home, more room for children."

The thought stirred her imagination. "Yes, I think my parents would like that."

"And somehow we'll save the old fireplace," he said, nodding toward the broad stone structure that stood resolutely while the burning embers sunk down lower and lower as the firemen doused the blaze with streams of lake water.

Finally Mickey voiced the concern that hovered around them both. "Where did Sam and Lorenzo go?"

"Looks like they took my car."

Mickey nodded. ''But I don't get it, did they just assume we'd die in the fire?''

''I don't think so. I think they left before it even started.''

''After all this they just left? This time they could have killed us. Surely they knew we'd get free eventually, or someone would come. They didn't know about the fire.''

''It was just an accident. I keep trying to blame them. But you know,'' he repeated in amazement, ''it was just an accident.''

''So why did they all of sudden just leave us? Even if they were doing something outside when the fire started you'd think they would wait to see if we got out. Just to be sure.'' She looked again into the shadows.

Alan shook his head. ''I don't know. I don't know anything anymore, except we are both alive, and we're together, and I don't think anything else matters all that much.''

''No. Not much.'' But still, she wanted to rid herself of the fear of Sam and Lorenzo forever. How could she do that if she didn't understand what they were trying to do, and why, and where they were? It became more and more confusing. She'd been missing something all along.

They were still standing side by side watching the last glowing embers when the police arrived.

Chapter Thirteen

The next morning a meeting took place in Alan's small office in the back of the copy shop. There were only two chairs, so everyone—Alan, Mickey, and Officer Chatillian—stood.

"Alan, your tormentors have most certainly departed," the police officer said after brief introductions. He was short and pudgy with dark eyes, prominent black eyebrows, and olive-brown skin. The uniform was immaculate, his salt-and-pepper hair was freshly trimmed and combed. "We have confirmation that two men with descriptions matching those you have given us flew to New York City late last night from Buffalo. They used different names, but we are sure it was them. In fact, a stewardess recalled that the small dark fellow had a large bandage upon his wrist.'' He waited, allowing them a moment to absorb this information, before continuing. ''I am afraid there is not much more that can be done. They have got away. It is unfortunate.''

''I'm just glad they are finally gone,'' Mickey said. ''That's a relief.''

''Can they get back into the country?'' Alan asked.

''We'll be on the watch for them, but certainly there are always ways. They are not foolish; they will not try using the same passports.'' He shrugged.

Mickey was crushed. ''I'll never be free of them, will I?''

''I cannot say for sure, Ms. Chapeskie, but with good luck they will not be back to trouble you. After all, they had their chance and they left of their own accord.''

Mickey nodded. ''Yes.'' They left of their own accord—that still puzzled her.

''There might be one way,'' Alan said, ''to be sure they never bother us again.''

Everyone looked at him skeptically.

''Have the police in São Paulo arrest them,'' Alan continued.

Mickey's hopes didn't have time to rise before they were crushed again.

''No,'' the police officer responded. ''It is pointless. We will advise our contacts with the São Paulo police of what has occurred here, but that is about all we can do. It is very difficult to extradite criminals from

Brazil. I have heard what these men did to you. And I certainly believe every word of what you say, but even attempted murder would be hard to prove. Extradition from a place like Brazil is very difficult even with a major offense and an ironclad case.''

"But what about a crime they committed in São Paulo?'' Alan asked.

"What?'' Mickey said.

"We do not—'' Chatillian started.

Undaunted, Alan carried on. "We never really discovered why they chased Mickey here and tried to kill her. Right? They didn't want to kidnap her and drag her back to Max, they wanted to kill her. It had nothing to do with that ring, did it? Then when they had the opportunity to finish the job, they left. Didn't bother with the ring, nothing.''

"They are crazy,'' Mickey stated, but even as she said that she knew it wasn't true. She knew them well enough to know they weren't crazy. "It's because we told them Max had died while they were here.''

"Really? They didn't know that? They didn't bother to verify it? They took our word that he was dead and just went home?''

No, Mickey thought to herself, that didn't make sense either. Would anything ever make sense? "They must have already known,'' she mumbled. "They wouldn't believe us.'' She spoke softly, tentatively, trying to make no assumptions. "It still doesn't sound right. It's as if they already knew he was dead, otherwise they wouldn't have believed us, but that wasn't important. What was important was that we knew.''

Officer Chatillian was confused. ''What did you know?''

Mickey was still working things through in her mind. *They went to great lengths to try to kill me, but when I told them something they already knew—that Max was dead—they just left me alone.*

Officer Chatillian still waited. Alan shrugged and explained, ''That Max had died.''

Chatillian glanced back and forth between them. ''You told them Max had died, but they already knew that. You said so yourselves. You did not tell them anything they did not already know.''

Mickey's voice rose. ''Yes, I did.'' Her voice became triumphant. ''We told them that Max had died! And they already knew he had died, but we told them, because we figured they didn't know.'' She went silent. ''We figured they didn't know,'' she repeated. ''We told them because we thought they might not know. What I really told them was, I didn't think they knew Max was dead.''

Alan grinned. ''That's what was important.''

Again Officer Chatillian glanced back and forth between them.

Mickey slipped back into the lush garden surrounded by a high stone wall behind a grand house on a hill overlooking São Paulo. She watched herself fleeing in her mind's eye.

She didn't look back, but she was keenly aware of the steady rhythm of the swimmer's splashes, listening for any break, any clue that someone had noticed.

She was running when she reached the back of the house. The rhythm broke. The splashes seemed to get loud, frantic, insistent. Mickey faltered, but no one yelled at her to stop. She listened, puzzled, but she didn't stop. Like a mountain climber refusing to look down, she wouldn't look back. Only an instant was lost. She hurried on.

Suddenly it was clear.

''They killed Max. They killed him, drowned him in the pool the morning I fled. They assumed I fled because I had seen the murder. They thought I was a witness. I kept telling them I didn't know why they were chasing me. I offered them the ring and told them they couldn't just kidnap me and take me back to Brazil. Then, when I told them Max was dead, they realized I hadn't seen anything, otherwise why would I bother telling the murderers that the person they killed was dead?''

''That's it.''

She had recognized how unusual it was for Louisa and Miranda to be out on the same morning, and how unusual it was for both Sam and Lorenzo to be in the pool pacing Max. It had all been arranged. She had even been alarmed when the swimmers' rhythm broke, she knew something had happened—she thought they had noticed her fleeing and were coming after her—

but she didn't look back, she carried on. That was the moment.

Mickey was trembling again. They were drowning Max when she was running away. That was what happened.

Officer Chatillian stated flatly, "But just knowing that that is what happened will not help—you said yourself you did not witness this murder. Hearing suggestive noises is very weak evidence, I think. In fact, you did not even know there was a murder until this moment. I am afraid they will get away with this."

"No," Alan interjected. "Surely if he actually drowned in a backyard pool, then was found in the ocean there will be some evidence, somewhere. Chlorine in the lungs, something."

"If they look." Now Officer Chatillian became excited. "And I will make certain they look."

"There will be other evidence too. In Max's boat, which they might have used to drop the body into the sea, or witnesses may have seen them loading a bag into the boat," Alan said.

"Lorenzo," Mickey snapped. "Sam was on the plane following me. Lorenzo didn't show up until later. He took care of the body."

"This will give the São Paulo police a lot to start with," Chatillian said. He was making notes.

Alan summed up. "Sam and Lorenzo killed Max. They thought Mickey ran away because she had witnessed the murder. I don't know, but they probably intended to kill her right after Max anyway. After all, she was just a foreigner, a woman alone, she'd be easy to kill and dispose of. When she fled, Sam chased her to silence the only witness. Lorenzo disposed of Max's body, making it look like a drowning.''

Mickey sank to a chair. ''That's it. It makes sense. That's why they've been trying to kill me.''

Silently they pondered the solution, seeking flaws. There were none.

Chatillian spoke directly to Mickey. ''I will need everything you remember about the morning you left Brazil, and we will forward it, and a few other facts, to the police in São Paulo. Then it is all in their hands.''

Mickey nodded.

''If we do it right away, they should be able to provide a little welcome-home party for your friends.''

''Okay,'' Alan said enthusiastically. ''I've got a lot to do here, so how 'bout you go with Jack to the police station and make out your reports. I'll be by to pick you up at eleven thirty and we'll have a picnic lunch in the park by the Champlain monument.''

By eleven forty-five they were seated on the edge of the town wharf with their bare feet hanging inches above the still blue water. It was a perfect day, and hordes of tourists wandered along the wharf and in the shade of the huge old chestnut trees. Lunch was finished. Mickey worked up the dregs of a boysenberry

Tempest. Again the nebulous status of their relationship had her feeling uncomfortable. There had been too much happening in their lives to allow them the tranquillity necessary to build on the breakthrough they had achieved the night before.

Alan seemed distracted, perhaps a little bogged down with a crush of chores. "So what now?" he asked.

"Well," Mickey said, "I was wondering, if you are not too busy maybe we could sort of celebrate and catch a movie sometime? My treat."

"Catch a movie?"

"Yes, like a date, you know."

"A date?"

"Yes, you know, sit in the dark and hold hands."

His interest piqued. "And hold hands?"

Mickey said softly, aware that he was teasing her, "Wouldn't you like to do that?"

"More than anything."

She decided to tease him right back. "I should warn you, I don't kiss on the first date."

"Well . . ." Alan laughed. "We'll see about that."

"Yes, we'll see."

"You know, the dating thing, I can sort of vaguely remember dating. It sounds like fun. When would be good for you?"

"Tonight?" Mickey asked.

"Tonight?"

"If that's okay?"

"I sort of had plans for tonight."

"Oh."

"Another time perhaps."

"Sure." He was teasing her. She heard it in his voice, saw it in his eyes. She wasn't sure what his game was, but she was willing to play. "What plans?"

"It's Friday. I was wondering if, before our company comes—"

She had forgotten about the company; how could friends come now, there was no cottage.

"—you'd like to get married this afternoon."

"We can't have company, we have . . . married?" She gasped.

"I've taken care of all that—tents and trailers. I own a small part of a car dealership with some other guys, so—"

"Married!"

"Why not? I'd hate to have to wait the whole weekend. I know a justice of the peace here in town, I phoned him this morning, he's ready. I phoned Luke, another friend who owns Cascade, a nice little jewelry shop, and Sylvia has a bridal service, she's—"

"Alan!"

"I'm sorry, I haven't done this exactly right, have I?" He slipped off the bench and sank to one knee. He no longer looked glib, quite the opposite; his eyes glistened and he looked as if he might cry. Suddenly she felt the same way. "Mickey Chapeskie, I've dreamed of this moment since the first day we met. Will you marry me?''

''Alan . . .''

''Today, five o'clock. I've spoken to Emile about catering a little reception—''

''It's so sudden.''

''No, it's not. We've known each other forever. We've been friends forever. I think we've waited long enough.''

''But Alan, it takes months to prepare for a wedding.''

''Yes, that's one way to do it.''

''There are guests to invite.''

''I know, I have a list of about seventy-five coming, but they are mostly just my friends, and your very old friends, but I thought we could fly out to L.A. or Vancouver and have another little reception or two for your sister and your friends next weekend, or whatever you want.'' He was still on one knee, both her hands encapsulated within his.

''But your businesses . . .''

''They do fine without me. Besides, I'd like to do some traveling, now that I've got the right someone to travel with.''

''But you can't arrange a wedding in three hours,'' she announced, instantly aware that he had.

''Are you saying no?'' He appeared crestfallen. His head dipped, but as he glanced back up at her the mischievous twinkle had sprung back into his blue eyes.

"I haven't decided yet," she said, lying.

He kissed her hands.

"You are so impulsive."

"It's my nature," he said with a laugh. "My new nature. Besides, I don't want you to get away again."

"You've thought of everything—except the honeymoon."

"Oh, believe me, I've thought of the honeymoon. It begins today and lasts forever."

Chapter Fourteen

Mickey stood on one ski and clenched her teeth. She dug in. Deep in the water the ski shimmied; only the tip was visible. She gritted her teeth even harder. Slowly she rose up. Then, as she skimmed along the surface, amazement flashed across her face in a radiant smile. She swung out over the wake, held the tow rope in one hand, then rocked, shifted her weight, and pulled in. A sharp turn. She created a shimmering curtain of water and shot back across the wake to the other side.

It had been a busy couple of days. A bulldozer and a backhoe were already cleaning up the burned debris of the old cottage. There was a tent trailer under the willow tree close by the water; that's where the newlyweds lived. Three other tents were scattered across the property for their weekend guests.

Sam and Lorenzo were gone and wouldn't be back—not for a very long time. The São Paulo police acted swiftly. They made the arrest at the airport, then they got lucky. There wasn't much in the way of concrete evidence, but Lorenzo confessed almost immediately and turned state's evidence in return for a lighter sentence.

Mickey switched the tow rope to her left hand. Her new diamond ring sparkled in the sun. She shifted her weight, gritted her teeth, and pulled hard. Another smooth veil of water shot up as she surged across the wake.